OVERDUE FOR LOVE

A LONG VALLEY WESTERN ROMANCE NOVELLA – BOOK 6

ERIN WRIGHT

WRIGHT'S ROMANCE READS

To my fans:
Thanks for helping make my dreams come true

PROLOGUE

DAWSON

June, 2008

*D*AWSON BLACKHORSE watched through narrowed eyes as Chloe Bartell sashayed toward the doors of the stable. He pretended not to notice the way she paused in the open doorway, giving him a deliberate look, and wiggled, a display that was emphasized by the short, tight denim shorts that barely encased her supple cheeks. Dawson was schooled at keeping his expression blank, but he couldn't keep his groin from tightening at the sight. Thankfully, he was standing in a horse stall that blocked her view of him from the waist down. He allowed himself a faint twitch of his lips at her annoyed expression as she flounced off.

As she stormed away, her ass cheeks bouncing as she went, he allowed himself to drink his fill of her lush frame. The sun sparkled off the long fall of blonde hair nearly touching her waist, along with the light copper hue of her skin, burnished to a warm sheen by the Arizona sun in which Chloe had languished all summer. Being the only child of a very rich father meant a whole lot of spare time to spend out in the sun in tiny bikinis and oversized sunglasses. Dawson had been able to spend a...considerable amount of time admiring that particular clothing combination.

With a curse, he turned back to the stall and began mucking it out again. If he dared to touch her, that'd be the end of his job *and* his chance to own the Bartell Ranch. Dawson paused for a moment and used a handkerchief to wipe the sweat from his brow, not sure if it was mucking the stalls or staring at Chloe that had caused him to sweat more.

He *had* to do something about Chloe before he gave into temptation. That would cost him everything. She was only twenty – a baby, really – and had always been sheltered by her doting and stupidly rich father. She was naïve and just had no idea what the world was really like.

Could she understand how much it meant to him to own the ranch? Could she understand that he might want her but that sure as hell didn't mean he could act on it? Hank had hired Dawson to work the ranch, and had even allowed him to work toward buying it someday, but he was under no illusion the other man would welcome a part-Navajo ranch hand into the Bartell family tree, any more than he'd welcome in a one-eyed, snaggletoothed possum.

Nope, Dawson had to keep his hands to himself, no matter how much she wiggled her ass at him.

With a curse that'd burn the hair off a hog, he turned back to the stall and began heaving the straw and manure into the wheelbarrow with a little more force than was necessary. If he couldn't screw himself into a stupor, he could work himself into one. For now, that'd have to do.

THE DAY PASSED in a blur of heat and manual labor, and it was a relief to finish around dinnertime. The heat of the Sonoran sun beat down on his shoulders as he made his way to the bunkhouse to grab a shower. It felt good to wash the sweat off and put on clean clothes before making his way to the main house, where Martha would have enough food to feed an army, or at least six hungry ranch hands.

With Hank's wife long gone, Martha had taken over the duties of feeding the ranch hands and the Bartell family, along with keeping up on the housework in the home. She refused to clean the bunkhouse, though, which Dawson couldn't blame her for. Going in there on a warm summer's day when no one had bothered to do laundry for a week…

The smell could get a little on the overwhelming side.

He found three of the other men seated when he entered, and the remaining ranch hands trickled in soon after. Hank and Chloe were last.

That was no surprise. Thank heavens Hank didn't make them wait for Chloe to show up before he allowed the ranch hands to eat. Either she wanted to make an entrance every night, or she had no idea how to read a watch.

Her hair – curled and hair sprayed within an inch of its life – and makeup so thick astronauts were checking it out, made it damn obvious she was no stranger to primping. Dawson was sure she'd look a sight better without all that junk smeared on her face and products plastered in her hair, but he wasn't about to tell her that. She was too gorgeous by half, and he didn't want to give her the idea that he was paying attention to her appearance. He wasn't sure how many more seduction attempts he could survive.

Not that she needed encouragement to keep

them going. When she took the seat across from him, she made sure she bent forward enough to guarantee he knew she wasn't wearing a bra under that skimpy tank top. His eyes cut sharply to the right and he made a point of looking at Martha as she bustled in from the kitchen with a big basket of biscuits. He could *not* stare at her.

Or her magnificent chest.

As Dawson ate, he pretended to be totally ignorant about Chloe's stares, or the fact that she was constantly shifting positions to better display her cleavage.

He was *mostly* successful, even when she slid her bare foot across his leg. His boots barred her from slipping her foot inside his jeans, but she was undeterred. His hand jerked and he focused on not spilling his coffee as her foot crept higher.

He cleared his throat, loudly, and shot her a warning look. Apparently, it was her turn to ignore him, because she looked away, but her foot kept moving upward.

He put a hand under the table to intercept

her foot, reaching for it a scant second after her foot reached its goal. He jumped, sloshing coffee everywhere. With a muttered curse, Dawson slid back his chair, using a napkin to mop up the spill.

"Sorry, Martha," he said as the house-keeper came to his rescue, dishtowel in hand.

She shrugged. "Just step back, son. Let me do my job." She was gruff but had a soft spot for all her "boys," as she called the workers. Though Martha looked nothing like his Navajo grandmother, who'd died three years ago, she reminded him of her in personality.

Dawson backed away, his gaze settling on Chloe. She appeared the very picture of inno-cence. He barely restrained himself from rolling his eyes.

Somehow, he finished dinner, aware of Chloe and Hank both watching him. The homemade strawberry cake stuck in his throat, and he gave up after three bites. "Thanks, Martha. Great dinner."

She waved off the compliments as the other men echoed Dawson. A scrape of the chairs and then he was falling into step with the others as they headed for the bunkhouse.

"Dawson?"

His stomach curled with dread when Hank spoke his name. He had no reason to be concerned, but he had a feeling Hank wanted to discuss more than tomorrow's chores. Pausing, he turned on his heel. "Yeah, Hank?"

"Come into my den, will you?" The invitation was an order, and they both knew it.

Dammit.

Dawson followed his boss into the man's den, ducking his head when he went through the door to avoid scraping it against the ornate frame. Hank sat down on a chair, indicating Dawson should take the wingback arranged at an angle across from his. He sat, trying to hide his reluctance.

Hank reached for the decanter on the side table, pouring a finger of whiskey into a crystal glass before handing it to Dawson. He took it but didn't sip the whiskey. Hank knew he didn't drink, but he persisted in pouring one for Dawson each time they had a serious talk –

which had been three times, counting tonight. First, when he'd promoted Dawson to ranch manager; the second time had been when he'd asked Dawson if he wanted to buy the ranch since Hank had no son to take over, and Chloe clearly wasn't interested.

The third reason? Well, that remained to be seen.

Hank sipped his whiskey before setting the glass on a coaster. Dawson did likewise, leaning forward slightly with his hands on his legs, trying to appear relaxed. "What can I do for you, Hank?"

"It's about Chloe."

His stomach churned. So, Hank had noticed Chloe's behavior. "I would never—"

"I can't give this ranch to anyone not in the family," Hank interrupted him abruptly.

"What?" Dawson wasn't keeping up with the topic shift.

Hank shifted his lanky frame, suddenly uncomfortable. "Bartell Ranch has been in my family since 1859, and it's going to stay with us."

"I'm not sure what you're trying to say to me," Dawson said slowly.

"The man who gets my ranch will be Chloe's husband."

He blinked, certain he had misunderstood. "What are you saying? You want me to marry Chloe?" The idea made his pulse quicken and his groin tighten. He'd been turning Chloe down for the last two years only because he didn't think Hank would okay a relationship between them. But if Hank wanted it, hell, Dawson was all over that.

Hank laughed heartily. "Hell no, Dawson. You ain't the right…man for her."

His eyes narrowed at Hank's hesitation, sure the other man had been about to say something besides "man." And then it hit him – the bigger implication. The more important implication than the fact that his boss was a racist.

"You aren't selling me the ranch, are you?"

Hank shook his head. "I'm sorry, son. I tried to get used to the idea, but I just couldn't. The ranch has to stay in the family."

Dawson absorbed the news with outward equanimity, though his insides twisted in anguish. He'd invested so much of his blood, sweat, and time into the Bartell Ranch that it was almost like someone had physically removed a part of his body. "What about our agreement?"

Hank shrugged. "I'll cut you a check for the money I've credited out of your salary. You should have enough to put a down payment on a nice little place."

Through gritted teeth, Dawson said, "I don't want some random little place, Hank. Bartell Ranch is my home. I wouldn't have worked so hard to get it back to its full potential if this wasn't supposed to be *my* ranch."

With a nod, Hank tipped back his glass, taking another drink before responding. "I know that. I'm not proud of it, but that's part of the reason I didn't tell you this before."

He'd hidden this from Dawson in order to keep Dawson working hard, stupidly believing…

Dawson pushed that thought away. He

couldn't deal with it head on, not now. Not yet. Later, when he could breathe properly.

"So, why now?" His voice sounded unfamiliar, cold and hoarse.

Hank contemplated his whiskey in his hand before finally answering. "Chloe'll be marrying King soon, and I won't need you anymore."

It was like a fist to the solar plexus. "She's getting married? To King Stedman?"

First off, *who names their son King?!* It was one of those white-boy things that Dawson would just never understand. Unfortunately, King didn't take the name as being an ironic choice, but rather as his parents bestowing a birthright upon him. He was the King of Cactus County, and didn't bother trying to hide that belief.

Hank nodded. "It's been in the works for a while now. The planning is over and all that's left is the wedding. I hope you didn't take her flirting seriously, son."

He closed his eyes, squeezing his fists to keep from lashing out at Hank. Chloe had spent the last two years trying to seduce him every time she was home from college.

Despite his best efforts, he'd started to think about her in a way…a way that he shouldn't have. And yet, she'd known that she was going to marry their closest neighbor? Dawson had thought Chloe was immature, sometimes shallow and spoiled, but he hadn't taken her for a liar or a cheat. Finding out what she was *really* like was almost as devastating as losing Bartell Ranch.

Dawson opened his eyes when he heard Hank stirring. Through shuttered lids, he watched the other man walk to the sideboard and open a drawer. When Hank came back, he was carrying a check he'd clearly prepared in advance. He took it without a word, knowing he would not be able to leave without an ugly confrontation if he started in on Hank's lies.

Well, it was easy to tell where Chloe had gotten her deceptive streak from. What was the saying – the apple doesn't fall too far from the tree? Rotten apples, the lot of 'em.

"You're welcome to stay a few days longer."

"I'll be leaving tonight," Dawson bit out, somehow holding himself in check. With reckless abandon, he lifted his whiskey glass and drained it in one swallow. "Give my congratulations to the happy couple." He stalked from the room, carrying a load of anger inside that felt like it would consume him.

CHLOE HEARD DAWSON LEAVING her father's den and positioned herself carefully in front of the opened door, making sure her ass was tipped high enough to give him a view of her... lack of underwear under her short denim skirt. If this didn't get his attention, she was giving up.

Of course, she'd made that same vow, and broken it, at least six times in the past two years, but she was going to ignore that fact. Right now, she *needed* him to pay attention to her. She'd wanted him for so long...

She stretched forward across the pool table, holding the pool stick to line up a shot. His footsteps outside the door made her stomach churn with nervous excitement, and she forgot how to breathe for a moment when he paused in the doorway. Knowing he was watching her sent a shiver through her, and the cue stick went wide, totally missing the shot she'd lined up.

"Hi," she said casually over her shoulder, ignoring her complete inability to play pool while he was in the room. She'd ignore it if he would. "You up for a game?" She was pleased by how nonchalant her voice sounded. She *almost* didn't sound like she was choking on her own heart from nerves.

He hesitated a moment longer before stepping over the threshold. The click of the door closing made her heart jump. "I've had more than enough of games today, Chloe."

His strange words and distant tone caught her attention. She set aside the pool stick and turned to face him. "Is something wrong?" She nibbled on her lower lip nervously. There *was* something wrong…

"I'm a fool."

"No," she said quickly and then stopped when he stepped closer, looming over her. Excitement warred with anxiety. There was something different about Dawson tonight. He wasn't aloof, and he certainly wasn't the indulgent, amused guy he occasionally allowed himself to be around her.

"Yeah, I was a fool to wait so long for this."

She gasped when he jerked her against him. Her body fit against his like she was made for the embrace. A colony of butterflies took flight in her stomach as she pressed her palms to his broad chest, feeling his steady heartbeat through the plaid fabric. "I agree," she said in a throaty purr.

Dawson's mouth covered hers, and she felt drawn into his heat. He consumed her, his presence overwhelming and absorbing her. Chloe's head spun as his tongue pushed its way through her lips, sweeping through the moist depths to conquer her. His lips seared, branding her as his, and she gladly surrendered, wanting nothing more than to belong to Dawson. *Finally*, she was getting what she'd wanted for the past two years.

And oh God, how it was worth it.

She tangled her hands in his dark hair, stroking the locks that were as silky as she'd imagined they would be. Dawson moved his mouth lower, nibbling along her jawline and down her neck. She whimpered when he breathed against the hollow of her throat, arching against him. He was hard and ready for her, the stiff length of him poking into her stomach.

Chloe gasped when Dawson cupped her ass and placed her onto the pool table. She tugged at the buttons on his shirt, eager to feel his bare skin against hers. Somehow, finally, her clumsy fingers managed to work the buttons loose so she could push the shirt off his shoulders, losing only one button in the process. She figured it was worth the sacrifice. She'd sew the damn thing back on for him later. Right now, she just had to feel his skin under her fingers.

She raked her nails through the crisp, black hair adorning his bronzed chest. "You feel so damn good," she murmured against his neck as she buried her face there.

He growled some kind of response that was

lost under the sound of her tank top ripping as he ruthlessly yanked it off. His large, rough hands cupped her breasts perfectly, and she arched her back to push them further into his hands. In her wildest fantasies, she couldn't have imagined just how good this would really feel.

And she'd had a *lot* of wild fantasies about Dawson over the years. She wondered for a moment if he knew how many times she'd imagined him in bed with her as she brought herself to orgasm. So tonight, maybe he wasn't in her bed, but she didn't care. She'd take him however she could have him.

Dawson's mouth replaced one of his hands, and he sucked her nipple into his mouth. Chloe cried out as he licked his way across her nipple, her body spasming. She didn't resist when he pushed her backward to lie on the pool table, stripping her skirt from her in the process. The felt of the table was slightly abrasive against her skin, but she completely forgot about that sensation when his mouth slid lower, leaving a wet trail down her stomach.

Her thighs clenched nervously as he tongued her belly button before moving farther south. Her stomach tightened with anticipation when he kissed it as he drifted to her warmth. She gasped as he breathed against her slit, the warm air making her feel a million sensations she'd never experienced before.

"Please, Dawson," she begged mindlessly.

"Please, what?" he asked, his chin propped on her belly, looking up at her. She craned her neck to look down at him and then dropped it back with a thunk on the table, groaning. She didn't know if she was asking him to taste her, or to just take her, or to not even put his mouth *down there*, for fear she would fall to pieces.

Chloe could only shake her head, leaving him to interpret her request. She didn't know what she wanted him to do; how could she tell him?

In the next instant, his mouth engulfed her as his tongue probed and explored. Chloe couldn't hold in a small cry when he swirled around and around. Her body burned, the fire originating from the epicenter of her. She writhed frantically, both seeking some kind of release while simultaneously never wanting him to stop.

"Please…" she whispered again, begging, wanting, not knowing what she wanted but begging mindlessly for it anyway.

Dawson plunged his tongue deep into her and then her body convulsed, arching against his mouth when he swept his tongue back up, sucking her bud into his mouth. The suction sent her over the edge, and she shuddered as she came, whimpering at the unbearable pleasure.

When Dawson lifted his head, his face was slick with her arousal, and he wiped it away carelessly with the back of his hand. Still without speaking, he pulled down his pants and lifted her closer.

Chloe bit her bottom lip as he slid inside her folds. Her body seemed to shrink in front of him. She hesitated, but he plunged deep inside her before she could say anything. Warn him. She should've told him back when they'd started this…this messing around, but she couldn't. She'd been so afraid he'd stop, and she'd waited so damn long…

And now she wished he would stop. She stiffened, surprised by how much it hurt. She'd expected some pain, but not *this* sharp. It ached and she bit down on her lower lip, trying to breathe through the pain. She would be fine. In just a moment, she'd be fine.

He frowned, staring down at her. "Are you —?" He broke off, just staring at her. She felt like a butterfly specimen, pinned to a felt board.

Embarrassed, she sat up and embraced him, burying her face against his chest. If she just didn't look him in the eye for a minute, maybe she wouldn't *actually* die of embarrassment. She had expected surprise, not…whatever it was he was feeling as he stared at her. Inscrutable – that was him.

She wiggled her hips against him and focused on relaxing her hips and stomach. She noticed the pain faded almost immediately. *That's better.* After an endless pause where Chloe tried to come up with the right words (*you can keep going now!* was all that came to mind, as tactless as that seemed), Dawson read her mind, withdrawing and thrusting back into her.

She winced at the flash of pain that, thank heavens, was at least a little milder than the first. By his third thrust, the ache had faded to a minor annoyance.

The cords in his neck were tight when she lifted her head from his chest. Enthralled by his expression, a mix of pleasure and anguish, she touched his cheek. He looked down at her, their gazes locking. His black eyes, normally hard and hooded, were softer, shining. Her lips trembled at the hint of vulnerability he showed, and she stroked his face, moaning when he pressed his mouth to the palm of her hand to kiss it.

She clenched her hands, breaking contact with his mouth, as he shifted positions to drive more deeply inside her. The pain returned temporarily, but pleasure soon washed it away, and she spasmed again around his length. Chloe arched her back, barely holding in a scream with her second orgasm that was even stronger than the first one he'd given her.

Her release seemed to trigger his, and he convulsed, pumping out his seed. He thrust as deeply as he could, resting his chin on her head as the last waves of ecstasy shook both of them.

Chloe had to resist the urge to lock her thighs around him and refuse to let Dawson break the embrace. Her stomach churned as she wondered if he would mention her virginity. Or lack thereof now.

She glanced up at him through the shield of her lashes, frowning when she saw his remote expression. Any hint of tenderness had disappeared. "Is something wrong?"

He shook his head. "Talk about a letdown. I waited two years for that?"

She flinched at his words, certain she must've misunderstood. "What?"

A sneer twisted his face. "You know *exactly* what I'm talking about. A virgin who has no idea how to please a man. I guess you screwed me over twice by also promising something you couldn't deliver."

Tears blurred her eyes, and she crossed her arms over her breasts defensively, letting her legs drop with a thunk against the side of the pool table. "Why are you being so cruel?" she whispered.

A cold laugh sent chills up her spine. "I'm being honest – something you and your father aren't familiar with, huh?" Dawson zipped up his pants, giving her one last dismissive look. "Your daddy screwed me, and now I've screwed you. I guess that makes us just about even." He turned and stalked out of the game room without a backward glance.

Shocked and wounded, Chloe eased off the billiards table to collect her clothes. The tank top was useless to her, but she was able to wrap it around her front enough to cover her breasts. She slipped on the skirt and rushed from the room, luckily not running into anyone as she made a mad dash to her bedroom. It wasn't until she'd locked the door behind her that she gave in to the sobs trapped in her chest. They escaped her with a choking sound, and she buried her face in her hands to muffle the noises.

Why had Dawson treated her so horribly? Why had he set out to hurt her when he must know she loved him? *Thought* she loved him. She could never love a man who would treat a woman like that.

Hurt and confused, she let the tears run their course. Eventually, Chloe dragged herself into the bathroom to run a hot bath. The water enveloped her, soothing the abrasions from the felt of the pool table, but doing nothing to assuage the hurt in her heart.

CHAPTER 1

DAWSON

NINE YEARS LATER
AUGUST, 2017

*E*ARLY ON A TUESDAY AFTERNOON, Dawson angled the horse trailer into an extra-long parking spot, straightening the wheels before killing the engine on the truck. He saw an eighteen-wheeler parked a few spaces over, but they were the only large vehicles there. Otherwise, only cars and small trucks occupied the restaurant's parking lot.

He locked the truck with the remote after

sliding from the cab. Bolt nickered when he peeked inside the trailer. "Hey, guy. I'll get you out of there soon." He knew the horse had to be restless after seven hours in the trailer. After an early start, it had been a *long* day and he was ready for some lunch.

After grabbing a bite to eat, he'd set up at the fairgrounds and let Bolt have some time outside. The horse was chomping at the bit to get out of the trailer, and Dawson could relate. He was eager to get this rodeo performance out of the way, so he could get off the road for a while.

His thoughts were heavy when he entered Betty's Diner. The Sawyer Stampede, set to start on Thursday evening, was the last rodeo of the season for him, even though there were several larger rodeos still to come. He needed a break from them all. Beyond that, he had no definite plans except to find somewhere he could hunker down and reevaluate.

With a shake of his head, he attempted to dismiss the thoughts as he took a corner booth away from the front counter. The stools housed cowboy-types, some looking authentic with dusty boots and frayed jeans, while others just dressed the part. The shine of their boots and immaculate dark-blue denim jeans gave them away – the typical rhinestone cowboys.

Dawson knew he'd present a puzzle to anyone trying to evaluate him. His cowboy hat and denim jacket were new, but dirt caked his black boots, and a seam on the side was coming undone slightly. His jeans were well worn, but his gold belt buckle would indicate he wasn't exactly scraping out a living working the land or tending herds.

Maybe they wouldn't have any trouble pegging him, he decided with a shrug. No doubt, Dawson stood out as a rodeo man, just like the others who would come into town over the next few days. Like him, they'd be gone by next week, and life would go on for the small town of Sawyer, the county seat in the Long Valley area.

Dawson started to lift his hand to get the waitress' attention, but his hand fell to the table with a jerk as a shock of recognition coursed through him. She wasn't looking his way yet, but he knew it was Chloe, even without her facing him. The short blonde bob and a well-worn pink waitress dress with a white apron were a far cry from the way he remembered her looking, but he had no doubts it was her.

Time had been good to her. She'd retained her lush figure, and her breasts had gotten fuller. From what he could tell, she had no visible lines marring her lightly tanned face. Time might have been kind, but clearly circumstances hadn't been, since she was waiting tables at a greasy spoon in an obscure Idaho town. He couldn't begin to guess what could've happened to have her end up here.

Just then, she looked up, holding up one finger to signal she'd be with him in a second. Her hand trembled, and her green eyes widened. The pad in her hand fell to the floor, and it took her a moment to bend over to retrieve it. When she did, one of the cowboys on a stool at the counter patted her on the ass.

Dawson was half out of his seat before

common sense returned. He had no claim on her and no right to be pissed that some stranger had touched her. For all he knew, the handsome young man wasn't a stranger. He might be Chloe's lover. His stomach heaved with nausea at the thought.

She smacked the cowboy on the hand, looking anything but playful. *Well, that rules lover out.* He couldn't hear what she told him from this distance, but the man dropped his head and appeared to mumble an apology. She went and ruined it by patting his shoulder, but he seemed more subdued when he lifted his head.

Dawson half-expected her to just ignore him, to leave him sitting in the corner booth until shift change, when he'd become another server's responsibility. To her credit, she squared her shoulders and approached him with a carefully blank expression, as though he was no different from any other customer.

"What'll it be?" she asked in a cool tone, positioning her body so he couldn't fully see her face. Or her nametag, he realized with a small smile.

"Coffee and the special." He didn't even have to look at the menu on the table to know this place had one. It was just like a thousand other diners in a thousand other small towns. Except this one had Chloe.

She repeated his order. "Anything else?"

"Yeah. When do you get off?"

She ignored the question and started to walk away.

"Chloe?"

At the sound of her name, she stumbled but regained her balance and kept walking to the counter. He couldn't help a small chuckle of amusement. He knew it was her, and she knew he knew it was her. No more pretending.

His mirth quickly faded when it sunk in that Chloe Bartell was in the same room as him, an event he'd thought would never happen again. It left a bad taste in his mouth to remember the last time he'd seen her. The memory of that evening…was not a pleasant one. She might've deserved to learn a lesson not to manipulate people, but the fact that he'd been the one to teach it to her so ruthlessly still didn't sit well with him whenever he thought about it — which wasn't often. Truthfully, Dawson did his best *never* to think about that night with Chloe.

She avoided his gaze when she returned with an empty cup and a half-full pot. The tremor in her hands was almost imperceptible as she poured the coffee.

Almost.

"Do I make you nervous, Chloe?"

Without a reply, she turned briskly on her heel and returned to the front counter, pausing to fill other customers' coffee cups on her way.

He tried to look away, but his gaze remained fixed on her as she bustled about, working while he waited for his special. It was almost surreal to find himself served by her. Who would have imagined there could ever be such a reversal in positions?

A few minutes later, she returned with an oval platter heaped with meatloaf, mashed potatoes, green beans, and Texas toast. "The special, sir."

Without thought, he grabbed her wrist as she turned to leave, shocked by the spark of electricity that surged through his hand. It was like touching a live wire. "Wait," he pleaded.

She stared over his shoulder, at the wall behind him, a determined set to her mouth. "Do you need something else?" she asked coldly.

"What time do you get done working?" he asked again. "We could grab a drink and catch up."

Chloe finally looked him in the eye, an expression of disbelief distorting her features. "You have some nerve, Dawson Blackhorse. I wouldn't want to 'catch up' with you if my life depended upon it. I just want to forget I ever saw you. My life is my business. You need to get the hell out of it, and get the hell out of Sawyer."

He frowned when she suddenly paled and swayed. "You okay?"

She tore her wrist from his grasp and rushed away from him, not looking back again as he ate the amazing diner food. Usually, diner food was all the same – prepackaged ingredients from the same food vendors that everyone used, but at least here, someone knew how to cook.

It was impossible not to watch her as he ate, though she never looked at him. It was fascinating to see the changes in her face and body – the same but yet completely different than her 20-year-old naïve self. She'd lost the pounds of makeup and hairspray, instead settling for a little mascara and lip gloss, and a light curl to the ends of her bob.

She looked…natural. Real. And somehow, so much more alluring than the 20-year-old version ever could have been.

Hmmm…she sure was looking at the clock an awful lot. Maybe it was almost the end of her shift, and she was just counting down the minutes until she could sneak out the back door and leave him behind.

With a sigh, he finished the last of his coffee, deciding he would leave cash on the table to avoid confronting her again. His presence upset her, and he didn't want that. She'd screwed him over, sure, but he'd gotten back at her and then some. The least he could do was leave her alone.

Dawson peeled a bill from his wallet and laid it on the table. He was busy pushing his wallet back into his pocket when he looked up in time to see Chloe glancing at the clock again, a look of relief on her face. She was damn happy to see him go. He tipped his hat slightly to her and started for the exit. It was time to leave her in peace.

As he reached to open the front door, it came tearing open on its own, almost whacking him in the shoulder. "Whoa, watch it, buddy," he said when he realized it was a little boy who'd come through the door like his tail was on fire.

Dawson reached for the door again just as the boy exclaimed, "Mom!" He seemed damn happy to see…

Hold on, Chloe is the only female in the restaurant. At least that he'd spotted.

He turned just in time to see the little boy hurl himself against her. It ripped through his gut to realize she had a family. Of course she did. And probably a husband too. A woman like her didn't stay single for years. She was too damn beautiful and rich to be single for nine years.

Well, maybe not rich anymore, but still damn gorgeous.

His gaze narrowed when he saw Chloe trying to turn the boy away from him, hiding him from Dawson's gaze. All he could make out was hair so black, it almost seemed to have a tinge of blue.

Then the kid squirmed out of his mother's arms, giving him his first look at the boy's face. Dawson sucked in his breath as he recognized the miniature version of the features he saw in the mirror every day. *His!*

He felt like he'd been punched in the gut. The world went in and out of focus as he tried to drink in every feature of the boy's face.

She curved a protective arm around his son, trying to draw the boy away. "Stop!" he demanded. Silence descended on the diner, and all eyes turned his way.

"I...I have to go, Betty," Chloe shouted, pulling the boy along with her as she disappeared into the kitchen.

Oh, she wasn't escaping that easily. Dawson ran out the front door of the diner, racing around to the back in time to catch her herding the little boy into a hatchback car that must be older than she was. Chloe bleated in terror at the sight of him, quickly closing her door and locking the car.

He reached the hatchback as she turned on the engine. Pounding on her window, he demanded, "Open up!"

She ignored him and shifted into gear, hitting the gas hard. Dawson lifted his fist, seized by the asinine urge to break the window. The look of alarm on the boy's face stopped him. He couldn't scare his son like that.

His son.

He watched her peel out of the employee parking lot, tearing over the curb and down the street, the taillights fading away. He just stared after her, frozen in place. With a shake of the head, he jogged back to his truck, determined to catch up with her before he lost her. Sawyer was a small town, but it could take a few days to track her down if he couldn't follow her car.

CHAPTER 2

CHLOE

"*M*ommy, who was that man?"

Chloe's heart twisted at Tommy's question. He hadn't called her 'Mommy' for a couple of years, so it showed just how frightened he was to have reverted to the more childish name. Licking her lips, she hesitated, searching for an answer she could give him. No *way* was she going to blurt out that Dawson was his father.

As far as Tommy knew, she had parted ways with his father before his birth, and before the other man had known about him. That was the truth, but she'd made it sound a lot more romantic – and a lot longer – than the one-night...whatever that was that she'd shared with Dawson.

Chloe snorted softly. *Shared.* Yeah, good one.

"Mommy?"

With a sigh, she said, "He's someone I used to know, honey. I just...uh...didn't want to talk to him again."

Tommy's eyes narrowed, and he appeared deep in thought. She continued driving, mentally crossing her fingers and hoping that would be the end of his questions. It took all her control to focus on the road in front of her while watching the rearview mirror for signs of an unfamiliar vehicle. Each time one appeared behind her, she tensed until it passed or she recognized the driver.

They were about a mile from the turnoff for home when Tommy asked in a tone just above a whisper, "Is that man my father?"

Chloe pretended not to hear him, keeping her attention on the road. How could she answer? Lying to him was unacceptable. She refused to do that. Yet, how could she give him an adequate answer that didn't involve confirming his startling perception? Running a hand through her short strands, she flicked on the turn signal and turned down the dirt road to the ranch house.

To her surprise, he didn't repeat the question even after she'd parked in front of the small house and shut off the engine. Maybe he sensed her reluctance to answer? Could it be that a part of Tommy didn't want to know? He was sensitive and intelligent enough to figure out that Dawson might not want to be part of his life even after learning he had a son.

And she couldn't imagine Dawson wanting any sort of role. Shock had propelled him to chase her, but she was pretty damn sure that he'd shun the idea once he'd calmed down. Besides, he probably already had a wife and family. They surely wouldn't want Dawson to bring home a bastard son.

Argh! Why did it make her chest ache to think about Dawson being married to someone else? It wasn't like she was still carrying a torch for him, obviously. After he'd laughed at her The Night on the Pool Table, as she called it in her mind, she'd grown up in a hurry.

She'd long ago realized that she hadn't loved Dawson – she'd lusted after him, but that was a typical kid thing to do. She hadn't known him well enough to love him, and what he'd done to her That Night killed whatever feelings she did have.

Despite her reassurances to herself about what her feelings did and did not include, her heart – traitor that it was – still thumped irregularly as she led Tommy through the warm, summertime air and into the house. Only mid-afternoon, they had lots of time to hang out and talk and read together like they usually did. The diner didn't bring in much of a paycheck but it sure was nice to work at a place that wasn't open past two o'clock. Normally, she helped with the clean-up duties for the day; she'd have to apologize to Betty for literally running out on her today.

So, I...uh...ran into a man today who I haven't seen in nine years, and last time I saw him, he took my virginity and threw it away like a used paper towel and then laughed in my face for giving it to him. Oh, and he knocked me up, too. Can't forget that part.

Yeah, that'd go over well. This was a story she was keeping to herself. She could come up with some other excuse to give to Betty tomorrow.

"Did Adam feed you lunch?" she asked, heading into the kitchen to find something to cook for dinner. Hopefully, the fridge had sprouted food that she hadn't noticed the last time she'd opened its door.

A girl could always hope, right?

Tommy rolled his eyes. "Of course, Mom. He made goulash." He grimaced. "Even his mother said it wasn't very good, but I ate it, 'cause I didn't want to be rude."

Chloe ruffled his hair with a smile. She sure was proud of her boy. "Good man. Now, run upstairs and grab a book you want to read together. I think we should start into *Where the Red Fern Grows* – do you think you can find that one on the shelf?"

Surprisingly, he complied without a peep of

protest. He usually tried to negotiate for a few minutes of video game time before giving up and looking for a book to read. Maybe he was taking it easy on her today, recognizing her stress. She may have had to grow up in a hurry, but so did Tommy. It wasn't easy being the only child of a single mother who was never quite sure where their next meal was going to come from.

She was staring into the fridge – no food having magically made its appearance, she was stuck debating between two meals, neither of which appealed to her – when she heard a vehicle coming down the dirt road.

It was almost anti-climatic, really.

Hoping for Adam Whitaker, or any of her close neighbors, she wasn't surprised to see an unfamiliar rig, with a horse trailer behind it, stop near her decrepit junker. Squaring her shoulders, she marched from the kitchen, letting the screen door slam behind her.

She made it almost to the porch steps by the time he slid from his truck. Chloe froze, the breath sticking in her lungs at his pure masculine beauty. There was nothing feminine about him, but beautiful was the perfect adjective. He'd grown into a solid frame. His hair was still glossy black, and she briefly imagined losing herself in the silky strands. How would it feel now?

Chloe blinked, trying to dismiss the carnal thoughts as she marched down the porch stairs, meeting him halfway. "Go away."

Dawson crossed his arms. "Not a chance in hell, Chloe. That's my son, isn't it?"

She nibbled on her lower lip, torn about how to answer. She had little compunction about deceiving the man who had so coldly rejected her, but it was useless to deny Tommy's parentage. He was a mini-me version of his father. "Yeah," she said with a sigh, shoulders slumping slightly.

"What the hell?" he shouted, sweeping the Stetson off his head. "You didn't think to tell me?"

"Lower your voice," she hissed. "Tommy's finding a book to read right now. I need to go upstairs to read to him. If you can be patient for a few minutes, we'll talk before you leave." She glanced pointedly at the truck.

He seemed on the verge of arguing, but the sound of Tommy calling her made him freeze. Dawson waved his hand, and she spun away from him to hurry back into the house.

Her mind was too busy to really focus on the first chapter of *Where the Red Fern Grows*, but Tommy didn't seem to notice. After finishing it, she kissed his forehead, and then said something she never said. "You want to play a video game?"

"Really?" he asked, bolting straight up, excitement shooting out of him like sparklers.

"Yeah. Just for a little while."

He bounced off his bed and shot straight for the guest bedroom that also had an old Playstation console in it that a friend had given them a couple of years ago. "Thanks Mom, you're the best!" he said as he disappeared from sight.

She smiled for a moment at the empty doorway and then stood up slowly. It was time to face the music. Descending the stairs, she drew in a few deep breaths, seeking to calm herself before facing him.

Chloe stumbled off the last step when she saw him sitting on her secondhand couch, a cup of coffee in hand. "Make yourself at home," she said sarcastically.

He lifted the cup. "Already did. I thought I'd make you some, too, since you so graciously invited me into your domicile."

His mocking tone set her teeth on edge. *How does a cowboy even know the word 'domicile'?* "You'll notice there was no invitation to enter my house. We can talk outside."

Eyeing her, he shook his head. "Nope, I don't think so. I wanted to see where the boy lives, and I'm comfortable here."

She wasn't. Having him inside the confines of the living room made the already small room shrink to tiny proportions. He seemed to suck all the oxygen from the air, making it hard to breathe. His invasion of her personal space was unsettling, but she decided not to argue, saving the energy for the rest of the conversation. Chloe took a seat in the threadbare wing chair farthest from him.

Silence lengthened between them. "Why didn't you tell me?" he asked after a long pause.

Chloe couldn't hold in a snort. "How was I supposed to do that? You disappeared. I didn't know where to even begin looking." She frowned. "I knew nothing about you. At the time, I didn't realize how little I knew, but it hit me afterward. I didn't even know your parents' names."

"Did you even try to find me?"

She glared at him. "Yes, you son-of-a-bitch, I tried to find you. You're a coldhearted, unfeeling man, but I thought you had a right to know." With a shrug, Chloe leaned forward to lift the other mug of coffee sitting on the scarred coffee table.

Dawson observed her through narrowed eyes. "I don't buy it."

The coffee scalded her tongue as she choked. "Excuse me?"

He smirked. "I don't believe you, Chloe.

Your father could've hired someone to track me down if you'd *really* wanted to find me." His mouth twisted. "I'm guessing you'd hoped to keep it a secret. Maybe you tried to pass him off as King's. It must've been a hell of a shock when he was born looking so damned Native," he said with bitterness. "Did it ruin all your plans?"

Chloe's mouth gaped open, and it took her a moment to remember how to speak, she was so angry. "Get out!"

"No," he replied blandly.

"I have had *enough!* I'm calling the police if you don't leave right now."

He set down the cup and crossed his arms. "Go ahead."

She glared at him, torn between the desire to get rid of him and the need to keep her private business private. Gossip was a town pastime in Sawyer, and she didn't want to add any more fuel to the fire. As it was, many of the older folks regarded her as a scandalous single mother.

"Why won't you just leave?" she finally

asked, hating the catch in her voice when she said it.

"Because we have a lot to talk about, starting with why you didn't tell me. Your father—"

Chloe interrupted him with a cold laugh. "Yeah, I'm sure he could've found you, but I didn't ask him. I couldn't. He wasn't eager to help me after learning about my terrible crime." She waved a hand wildly around the dilapidated living room. "My father has nothing to do with the *grand* life I'm accustomed to living these days. I haven't seen him in almost nine years."

He frowned. "What happened to the joining of dynasties and your marriage to King?"

She leaned forward to put the mug back on the table. She didn't dare keep it in her hands – she was so pissed, she was liable to slosh it everywhere. "Nothing. No one bothered to ask *me* if I wanted to marry him. My father arranged it all."

Dawson went pale. "You…you didn't know?"

"Of course I didn't know." She glared at him. "I know you have a low opinion of me, but I guarantee you, I wouldn't have been chasing after you like such a pathetic little puppy if I were engaged to King." With a twist of her lips, she added, "Not that you'll believe me, but quite frankly, I'm beyond caring what the hell you think of me."

To her surprise, he didn't respond. Instead, Dawson stared down at his worn cowboy boots, looking lost in thought. When he finally looked up, the regret visible in his expression made her heart hurt a little.

Just a little.

"I'm sorry," and dammit all if he didn't actually sound sincere. Her heart hurt just a little more, a fact she was hell bent on ignoring. He sighed. "Your father said the only thing left to do was the wedding. It seemed like you'd known all along. I was angry at what he'd done, and at what I thought you'd done. I shouldn't have—"

"No, you shouldn't have," she cut him off angrily. "But, whatever. I don't know what happened between you and my father and honestly, I don't care. I have more important things to worry about these days." She glanced at the clock on the wall. "Now, if you're finished with this trip down memory lane, you need to leave. I have to tend to the animals before it gets dark, figure out what to make for dinner, and decide what the hell I'm going to tell my son about the crazy man at the diner today.

"It's been a hell of a long day, and quite frankly, I just want to crawl into bed." Lest he think she was issuing one of her gauche teenage invitations she'd so blatantly dispensed years ago, she added, "Alone," in a steely tone.

He seemed on the brink of arguing, but finally nodded. "This isn't over."

"Yes, it is." Exhaustion and emotional turmoil were creeping up on her, making it difficult to stand, let alone continue the verbal sparring. "There's nothing left to discuss."

Stetson in hand, Dawson headed for the exit through the kitchen. She followed, making sure he actually left the house. When he paused in the doorway, she gulped, not liking the expression of determination he wore.

"There's plenty to talk about, starting with me becoming part of my son's life."

"*My* son," she said in a fierce whisper. "*You* have nothing to do with it."

He pushed the hat firmly on his head. "I have everything to do with it. You don't have to bear it all alone anymore."

"I don't want your help." She turned her head away when he brushed his fingers down her cheek.

"What we want doesn't really matter anymore. All that matters is our son. Tommy?" He sighed when she wouldn't look at him. "We'll talk again soon."

Chloe took great pleasure in slamming the door behind him and locking both locks. If only it were as easy to keep him out of her life as it was to keep him out of her house.

CHAPTER 3

CHLOE

THE ALARM WOKE HER MUCH TOO EARLY. She had lain awake most of the night, her mind a jumble of fearful and confusing thoughts. Sometime near dawn, she had come to the decision that she and Tommy would have to leave Sawyer and start over somewhere else, where Dawson couldn't find them. It would be painful to leave their friends, but not as painful as it would be to have him interfering with her life, trying to take over.

She hit snooze on the alarm, deciding the animals could wait a few more minutes. She would skip on makeup to indulge in a couple of

snooze sessions. Her eyes closed almost immediately, and she slipped into a deep sleep.

A couple of hours later, Chloe bolted
straight up, knowing the position of the light
streaming through her window was all wrong.
It must be late. She looked at the clock and
groaned. With luck, Betty would be in a for-
giving mood, because she was going to be late.
There was no way to take care of the animals,
shower, and drop off Tommy at the Community Center Day Camp and make it to work in
fifteen minutes, when her shift should begin.

She dragged herself from bed, cursing at
oversleeping and at Dawson for wearing her
out so much with worry that she had slept
through the snooze alarm. Slipping into jeans
and a flannel shirt, she shoved her feet into
rubber boots and trudged down the stairs. On
her way past Tommy's door, knowing he must
still be asleep since he hadn't woken her up, she
shouted, "Wake up, sleepyhead. We need to
leave in thirty minutes." They'd only be able to
leave then if she could just milk and feed the
cow and goat, *plus* gather the eggs and feed the

chickens, *plus* squeeze in a shower, all in a half-hour. Okay, fine, unrealistic at best, but she really didn't have a choice.

Chloe stumbled to a stop when she saw the buckets of milk on the kitchen table. Wearing a frown, she rushed outside, wondering if Tommy was up and had slipped out to milk the animals. She'd already told him countless times that he was too young. Skunk – named by Tommy when he was so young, everything black and white was a skunk – was a placid enough cow, unless one yanked her udders the wrong way. The old girl wasn't above kicking.

Her heart stuttered in her chest as she pictured Skunk kicking Tommy, knocking him unconscious. He could've died.

Well, obviously, he didn't since he'd gotten the pail of milk onto the table, but that didn't keep her from imagining it all in great detail in her mind. And Ivy! There were *two* buckets on the table. He'd milked the goat? She was ornery as could be and was just as liable to stand still as she was to head butt and kick.

Now in a high state of panic, she went running down the porch steps and across the yard before freezing at the sight of Dawson's truck parked in her driveway. She looked at the corral, surprised to see a chestnut horse sharing space with Skunk the cow and Ivy the goat. Her eyes narrowed with anger as she searched for her uninvited guest.

Her heart skipped a beat when she heard Tommy's high-pitched voice coming from inside the chicken coop. She hurried to find her son, her mouth dry when she saw him standing so close to Dawson, a look of admiration on his all-too-grown-up face. He held a basket while Dawson gathered the morning eggs from the indignant chickens.

When Tommy saw her, he beamed, waving his arm frantically. "Mom, look, Mom." He held up the basket. "Me and Dawson collected the eggs and milked Skunk. Ivy tried to get away, but we caught her and milked her too." He grinned up at her as she approached. "Dawson let me carry the buckets into the house."

"That's nice." She glared at Dawson over

her son's head. "You should call him Mr. Black-horse though."

Tommy stuck out his lower lip and crossed his arms over his chest, the basket dangling from his hand. He looked so much like his father, her heart twisted in her chest. It was the same look Dawson had given her just last night.

"Dawson said I could call him Dawson, Mom. It'd be rude not to call him Dawson when he said to call him Dawson."

She sighed, letting it go. "Okay, little man." With a hug around his shoulders, she said, "Could you take the eggs up to the house and put them in the egg keeper? I need to talk to Dawson."

"Sure!" His eyes sparkled with the responsibility. He grasped the basket and ran toward the house at breakneck speed.

Chloe managed to contain her anger until she heard the sound of the screen door slamming behind Tommy. "Why are you back?" she demanded.

He had the gall to only look somewhat ashamed. "Well, I left for town for a while, figuring that'd give you enough time to make dinner and do the evening chores, and then slipped back here after dark. I put Bolt in the corral and bedded down in my trailer for the night."

"What do you want?"

"My son."

Her eyes widened, and the panic she'd only just managed to shove down came roaring back. "Over my dead body! You can't just come into his life and try to take him—"

"Whoa." He held up a hand. "Hold on. I meant I want to get to know him. I'm not trying to take him away."

She continued to glare at him for a moment longer. "You'd better not even *think* about having the faintest idea of doing so. I would do anything for my son, including kill."

His lips twitched, but he at least had the good sense not to laugh. Out loud, anyway. "I just want to spend some time with him and help you out. Ease your burdens."

"Where were you when I *wanted* your help?" She swallowed the urge to scream and stamp her foot. "You know, whatever. It doesn't even matter. The only thing that matters is Tommy." She poked him in the chest with one finger. "Just make damned sure you're prepared to stay in his life to some degree if you decide to spend time with him. It's better for him to never know his father at all than to have you for a few days before you just up and disappear." Chloe sneered at him. "We both know you're good at that, don't we, Dawson?"

Before he could answer, she whirled around and headed back to the house. Tommy met her halfway, and she said, "Go wash up and get dressed. We're going to be late as it is."

His face fell. "Aw, Mom, I wanted to spend the day with Dawson."

She shook her head. "I'm sure Mr. Black-horse has other things to do, and they're expecting you at the day camp."

"But—"

"Besides, Adam and his mom would miss having you for lunch."

Tommy scuffed the toe of his sneaker in the dirt. "I guess."

She took a deep breath, relieved not to have to deal with an argument. "Let's get ready."

"Will you be here tonight, Dawson?" asked Tommy eagerly.

"No," said Chloe.

"Yes," said Dawson.

She gritted her teeth.

"Yes," Dawson repeated, ignoring Chloe. "I'll be here for a few days, at least. I'm supposed to compete in the rodeo, but I don't have any other plans." He shot her a glance of amusement. "I'm all you and your momma's for a while."

Tommy pumped his fist in the air. "Awesome." He turned to run into the house, finally deciding to get dressed, apparently.

She growled, finding it almost impossible to keep from yelling. "What do you think you're doing?"

Dawson grinned, and his teeth were just as white and straight as they'd been nine years ago, looking so beautiful against his coppery skin. "I'm pissing you off by inviting myself to stay with you for a few days."

Arrggghhhh!

Rendered speechless by her rage, she spun away from him and marched into the house, hoping a shower would clear her mind a little and allow her to at least have a conversation with the annoying man invading her life. One that he *didn't* win.

CHAPTER 4

DAWSON

*D*AWSON HELD IN HIS CHUCKLE until he was sure she couldn't hear him. From the flames practically shooting from her eyes, a blind man would've been able to tell she was damn livid. If she knew he was amused, she'd likely slug him. Of course, he'd have to stop her before her hand could connect. Then he'd take her into his arms and…

With a sigh, he tried to dismiss the thought. The strong attraction to Chloe took him by surprise. Knowing she hadn't lied to him wasn't what brought it back. It had been smoldering just below the surface ever since he spotted her in the diner yesterday. One look at Chloe and he was back to feeling like he'd grabbed hold of a live wire.

He sighed again, taking off his Stetson to run a hand through his hair. His attraction to Chloe was the least of his concerns. Or, at least it should be. *He had a son.* Even after lying awake most of the night, staring at the ceiling of the horse trailer, he still found it almost impossible to believe he and Chloe had created a life.

A life she'd had sole responsibility over for the last eight years.

He winced. The last thing he'd ever wanted was to ruin her life.

He'd been pissed as hell that last night, and in a vengeful mood, but not *that* vengeful. Not like that.

Rational thought just hadn't entered into the equation. He'd thought with his fury and his zipper, not his brain. He shook his head at his stupidity. All these years, it hadn't even occurred to him that she could've gotten pregnant from it.

In all fairness, if he'd considered the idea, he probably would've just assumed that she'd "handle" it if something like that had happened. It had seemed so clear that she was going to marry King and had been leading him on. It had never occurred to him to question that.

It had never occurred to him to ask her questions.

Cursing under his breath at his stupidity – all nine years of it – Dawson went over to unhook the trailer from the truck. Chloe was going to be pissed – even more so than she already was – but he was going to drive them into town. No way was she leaving his sight now that he knew about Tommy. He still didn't trust her not to take the boy and run away. Chloe hadn't yet grasped that he had every intention of living up to his responsibilities. He would've done it nine years ago, *if* he'd known about the baby.

He grimaced, thinking about how much of his son's life he'd missed. The boy was a stranger. And after all this time, Chloe was a stranger too. He guessed she'd always been a stranger to him. Lust. That was what they'd had between them when he'd worked for Hank, that's all they had between them for two long years. Two long years of never touching, and then…spontaneous combustion.

And she hadn't known him either. Even after he'd worked for her dad for years and years, she'd still had no clue where to start looking for him when she'd left Hank's.

Dawson growled low in his throat. Left, or had the old man kicked her out when she hadn't lived up to his expectations? It was another question to add to the list he was mentally putting together. He was going to sit her down – staple her ass to the chair if need be – and get her to answer some questions the next chance he had.

He saw them heading towards the car and intercepted them. "How about I drive you today?" he asked casually, staring Chloe straight on.

"No!" Chloe said emphatically, even as Tommy was running to his rig.

"Whoa, Mom, look at this," he called out, opening up the door and staring inside. "It's even nicer than Doc Whitaker's truck."

She trudged towards the truck, resignation in every step. Dawson grinned to himself as he headed to the driver's side. Yup, going through Tommy was definitely the way to get Chloe to do something.

"It sure is something," said Chloe, clearly reluctant as she climbed into the cab after her son. Judging from her body language, the Ford might as well have been a torture chamber.

Dawson climbed inside and suppressed a groan, discovering it really could be a torture device. He was so close to Chloe and her tantalizing scent, and yet, he couldn't touch her. He checked Tommy's seat buckle to make sure he'd properly strapped himself in on the bench seat, a much-needed buffer between him and Chloe.

"Everyone ready?" he asked, bringing the diesel engine to life.

"Yeah," said Tommy, practically bouncing. Chloe didn't bother to answer, so he took her silence for assent and put the truck in gear. He couldn't deny a twinge of nerves as he wondered what the day would bring.

CHAPTER 5

CHLOE

CHLOE SHOT A BALEFUL GLANCE AT DAWSON, sitting at the stool farthest from her, tapping away on his laptop. He'd come in with her after they dropped off Tommy. First, he'd ordered breakfast, and then coffee, pie mid-morning, followed by lunch during the rush. He wasn't sitting around or loitering, so she couldn't ask Betty to kick him out.

Especially since the older woman found him so damned charming. Dawson had poured it on thick with Betty and May, the other waitress, and after what seemed like only minutes, he had them laughing girlishly and flirting shamelessly. Never mind they were both old enough to be his grandmother.

Deputy Connelly, or just Abby to her friends, came walking in just then, a big smile on her face as always. It was her job to pick up the lunch meal for the inmates at the Long Valley County Jail and it was usually the highlight of Chloe's day. Abby was a kickass friend and someone who could always cheer her up.

She was pretty sure Abby was going to fail today.

She sent her a beleaguered smile, doing her best to appear happy, and failing miserably.

Abby slowed her pace, her nightstick swinging on her hip when she came to an abrupt halt. "Hey, girlfriend," she said slowly. She leaned on the counter and looked up at her, confusion writ large. "The Sawyer Stampede is this weekend, and this town is full of hot cowboys, all of whom are going to stop by this cafe. How are you not dancing on the ceiling about this? Or at least have a little bit of drool wandering down your chin?"

Chloe could *sense* Dawson's extreme interest in this conversation, even as he pretended to be looking intently at his laptop. She called bullshit.

Abby caught the flick of her eyes down to Dawson and back again, and, leaning forward a little too obviously, checked him out. His dark skin, his long silky black hair, his muscles bulging everywhere, stupidly sexy…

She viciously stomped that thought out. She wasn't going to let Dawson's muscles, sexy or otherwise, enter her mind. He was just another patron. A customer of the restaurant, and someone who Abby was making a fool of herself over.

"Speaking of," Abby breathed quietly. Dawson's mouth quirked. Chloe thought about throwing her washrag at his head.

"Are you ready to pick up the lunch for the inmates?" she asked Abby loudly, wondering if she was going to have to get a stack of napkins so she could mop up the drool about to collect in a puddle under Abby's chin.

"Yeah, sure," Abby said absentmindedly,

still staring at Dawson. Chloe marched to the kitchen, grabbed the prepackaged meals, and brought them back out to the front counter, shoving them into her face. This jerked Abby back to reality and she looked up at Chloe with a laughing grin on her face.

"Well, it looks like you have…a lot on your hands, eh? Give me a call later and tell me about…everything you've been up to."

She had a half a mind to chuck her washcloth at Abby's head instead as she headed back out the front door, meals in hand, whistling innocently as she sauntered out into the sunshine, but knew that Dawson would just take that as a victory.

And he most definitely had *not* won.

She returned to wiping the already clean front counter, not looking up again until she heard May giggling. She was ostensibly pouring Dawson another cup of coffee, but the pot sat on the counter, while the other woman leaned across it to talk to him.

She definitely wasn't jealous of the attention he gave the women. Obviously. She'd have to like someone to be jealous. Chloe just found their behavior…absurd. Ridiculous, even.

She scrubbed hard at the counter.

At least she'd made it through most of the day without having to talk to him or even look his way. They'd traded a few words, but she'd managed to keep herself busy with tasks that kept her well away from him.

It irked her to no end that she had to give him a chance to get to know Tommy. There was no way in hell she was giving him a chance to charm her again, though. Chloe snorted. As if that were possible.

"Got a cold, hon?" asked Betty, a knowing gleam in her eyes.

Chloe mumbled something along the lines of, "Wlkdnsesnd," and continued polishing the counter.

No, she didn't know what that meant either. That was kind of the point.

"You're going to wipe the white clean off that tile if you keep scrubbing, Chloe."

With an annoyed grunt, she lifted the damp cloth and then stared at it balefully. She'd run out of things to do and her boss wasn't helping matters. This was the perfect day to clean out the fryers – in the kitchen, far, far away from Mr. Dawson Blackhorse who seemed to have molded his ass to the bar stool at the front counter – but Betty had told her no when she'd suggested it.

The ringing phone saved the day, and she snatched it up a little too aggressively, barely keeping her voice pleasant when she said, "Betty's Diner, how may I help you?"

"Chloe, it's Adam."

"Oh hi!" She smiled. Adam was her best friend and usually cheered her up just with the sound of his voice. "What's up?"

"I just picked up Tommy, but I've got a call from Stetson Miller. One of his cows is feeling poorly. Is it okay if I take Tommy with me for the call? I'd drop him off by the diner or at home with Mom, like usual, but we're really close to the Miller's. I can bring him home after."

"Sure, that'd be fine. Thanks, Adam."

When she hung up, Betty asked, "Every-thing okay?"

Chloe nodded. "Yeah, fine. Adam wanted to know if he could keep Tommy long enough to make a house call. The youngest Miller boy has a sick cow."

With a speculative look at Dawson, the other woman said, "Why don't you take off early, girl? It's dead around here — the rodeo ain't started yet — and, well, I'm sure you can think of a way to fill the time before Tommy gets home. His daddy will probably have a few ideas."

She jumped, shocked that Betty had recognized Dawson as her son's father. It was stupid to be surprised, since they looked so much alike. She'd just sort of hoped no one would have eyeballs. Or use their eyeballs. Or at least restrain themselves from mentioning the fact that they'd used their eyeballs. "That's not necessary," she said, emphasizing every word.

Betty took the damp cloth from her hand. "Sure it is. Why should I pay you to stand around doing nothing?" She chuckled, raising her voice as she looked in Dawson's direction. "Young man, why don't you give this lady a ride home?"

With a big grin, Dawson shut his laptop and stood up.

Fuming, Chloe stripped off the white apron and tossed it into the box under the counter. "Thanks, Betty," she said through gritted teeth.

"Anytime," said the other woman serenely, as though she were completely oblivious to Chloe's true feelings.

It was too damn bad Betty was her boss; she had a whole *string* of words to say if she wasn't. "Have fun," Betty added with a big grin.

"I'll see you tomorrow," she ground out, ignoring Dawson as he came up behind her.

"It's okay if you're feeling sick and can't come in." Betty winked at Dawson as she spoke.

"I'll be here, right on time," said Chloe through a forced smile.

Betty waved a hand. "Get on outta here."

The gentle affection in her tone was sweet, as always. Betty was sweet. Betty was a good boss.

At the moment, Chloe just couldn't bring herself to care. Without looking at either one of them, she headed out into the bright, August sunshine.

CHAPTER 6

DAWSON

IRED OF THE SILENCE IN THE CAB, Dawson decided to ask Chloe some of the questions he'd been wondering about all morning. He'd even written them down in his laptop, so he wouldn't forget them all, but that didn't do a bit of good while he was driving.

He could always start with the obvious one though, and see where it went. He could pull out his laptop later.

"Why aren't you still living at home with your father?" he asked, breaking the silence. "He would've been able to help you and

Tommy live…well, a lot easier than the salary of a waitress could afford you."

She seemed to just ignore him, staring out the window at the passing pine trees. When the silence became awkwardly long, Dawson sighed. Time to think of another question. Maybe he could break the ice and work his way towards the important stuff.

And then she spoke. "He didn't want me to have Tommy," she said softly. "He offered to pay for the abortion so I could still marry King." She snorted. "As if I would've done that. When I refused, he started threatening me. He was going to disown me and ruin my life."

Dawson had to grind his teeth together to keep from revealing how much her words angered him. "What happened?"

She shrugged. "He locked me in my room. How medieval is that? I heard him on the phone beforehand, arranging for a private doctor. That bastard was going to bring in someone to kill my baby against my will."

His knuckles were white on the steering wheel. "I wish I'd been there for you."

Chloe ignored that and kept going. It was like she'd been dying for years to get this off her chest. And, maybe she had. "Ruth found out what he was up to and let me out, bless her. I took what I could carry and stopped at several ATMs, until I'd taken out all the funds my accounts allowed for the day." A harsh laugh escaped her lips. "Sure enough, Hank had frozen my checking and credit card accounts by the next morning."

"How—" He croaked before clearing his throat. "How much did you have?"

"Three thousand. I had three thousand dollars to live on, with no job skills." A hint of fear laced her words, as though she still recalled the panic today.

"How did you end up in Idaho?"

"I used the Mustang Hank had given me for my eighteenth birthday to get to Phoenix. Since he'd threatened to cut me off from everything, I figured he wouldn't be above reporting the car stolen. I parked it at the airport and took the bus to one of the seedier car lots, figuring I could afford something there. I bought the car I'm driving now."

Imagining her driving around in that relic, especially when she'd been pregnant, made Dawson flinch. Hank hadn't had to ruin her life. Dawson had beaten him to it by leaving her pregnant and alone. "So, why Idaho?"

Her head fell back against the headrest. "I remembered you saying something about a cousin in Washington, so I was driving there." She sniffed. "It was a stupid plan. I didn't even know your cousin's name. He might not have been a Blackhorse. In hindsight, I can't believe I was so foolish." After a pause, she said, "Anyway, I stopped and worked as I went along, getting together as much money as I could. A couple of times, I stayed in by-the-week motels. Once, I spent two weeks on a bartender's couch. He and his girlfriend felt sorry for me. I stayed with them until the owner decided I was showing too much. Pregnant waitresses must make drinkers uncomfortable." She gave him a small smile, but it quickly disappeared. "Mostly, I lived in the car."

Unable to hold back, Dawson cursed a blue streak. "I'm so sorry, Chloe."

Again, she ignored him. "I made it to Sawyer when the car broke down. It was the middle of March and snowing like crazy, and I was eight-and-a-half-months pregnant on the side of the road."

He glanced over, worried by her pallor. Maybe he shouldn't keep pushing her for answers. Did it really matter how she'd ended up here? Well, yeah, it did, but not at the expense of causing her more pain. "It's okay. You don't have to finish," he said, trying to reassure her.

Chloe leaned forward and glared at him. "Yes, I do. You need to know what happened after you screwed me and ran. Maybe then you'll understand why I want you to drive off and keep going, never to come back."

He swallowed, managing a tight nod. *Okay, I deserve that.*

"I started having contractions. At first, I thought they were just Braxton-Hicks, which

I'd had off and on for a few weeks. But they kept getting worse, and then my water broke." She pressed on, talking over the hissing sound he made before he could stop himself. "I thought I was going to be delivering Tommy myself in that car. You have no idea how terrified I was."

"I can imagine," he said in a whisper.

"Not really," she volleyed back, and Dawson nodded. *Okay, I deserved that, too.* She seemed to let it go, though, and continued. "If it hadn't been for Doc Whitaker seeing my car and stopping to check on me, I don't know if we would've made it."

The name sounded familiar. "Is he the one Tommy's with?" She nodded, making his stomach clench. Was this doctor her boyfriend? And did he have any right to care if the doctor was? At least the man had been there when she needed him, which was more than Dawson could say about himself. He tried to keep any trace of jealousy from his voice when he spoke. "Imagine the odds, a doctor stopping when you were stranded."

Chloe laughed, this time without a hard edge. "Adam is a vet. I think he was almost as scared as I was when he delivered Tommy." She grinned, her expression soft with affection. "He told me he hadn't had kids by then and never would, thanks to that experience."

He forced himself to chuckle, even though he felt like he'd swallowed a live snake. *She loves him. Just look at the way her eyes light up when she talks about him. You're too late, Dawson. About nine years too late.*

"He helped me give birth in his new truck. Afterward, he wrapped up Tommy and me in a horse blanket and spent the night keeping us all warm and making sure we were okay. In the morning, the snow finally stopped, and he took me to the hospital over in Boise. They released us within hours, and Adam took us home with him. He lived with his mother, Ruby, and I was afraid she'd feel differently than he did about charity for strangers. Thankfully, she adored Tommy from the start." Chloe smiled again, her expression full of affection. "I wish their cats had felt the same. They took a while to come around."

"I'm glad he helped out." That sentence came out normal-sounding and genuine. He was tempted to pat himself on the back for that. The truth was, he *was* happy the good doctor was there to help out. He just wished he had been, too.

She nodded. "So am I. Adam introduced me to Betty, and she hired me. Ruby watched Tommy for a long time, until her arthritis got too bad to chase after him. Luckily, he got old enough to start attending school, and so now Adam helps Ruby with Tommy after school. During the summer, he goes to the day camp at the community center. It's nice that the diner closes at two o'clock every day – I don't have to worry about trying to find babysitters in the evening."

Relief swept through Dawson as he pieced together what she *hadn't* said. Bad arthritis must mean his mother was elderly. The vet lived with his mom and some cats, and he'd never had kids. He barely suppressed a smile. Whitaker was probably middle-aged, maybe even gay. Certainly not any competition for him to worry about. That was one less problem to overcome on the path of getting Chloe back.

The urge to smile vanished with the thought. *Hold your horses there, Dawson.*

He wasn't trying to get her back. They'd never really been together. He just wanted to be part of his son's life and help Chloe. That didn't equate to having a relationship with her. Since she was the mother of his kid, having an affair with her just didn't seem right, so…

Hands off, buster.

He gripped the steering wheel tighter, his knuckles turning white with the strain.

As they pulled onto the farm's dirt driveway, he asked, "How'd you end up living out here, so far away from town?" It made him nervous to think of Chloe on her own with only Tommy there with her, and miles from help if something happened.

"Adam again. This was his place. He bought it and lived here with his wife until she died. Then he moved in with his mother to take care of her, with her arthritis and all. She refused to leave her house, so the farm just sat here, unused. It was hard for him to take care of his mom *and* the farm *and* be a full-time vet, so it was getting neglected. He lets us stay here for free in exchange for taking care of the property and the animals."

Her explanation added another dimension to the doctor. So, he wasn't gay – *dammit* – but he was a widower. Definitely middle-aged and obviously too old for Chloe.

Again, not something he really cared about, right? Right.

Rrriiiggghhhhttt…

He ignored that thought, too.

He pulled to a stop and she hopped out of the truck before he could think of an appropriate reply that didn't include the words "How old is he?" or "Are you in love with him?"

"If you're going to hang out here," she tossed over her shoulder as she headed towards the house, "you can make yourself useful. You go milk the girls again while I start dinner." Without waiting for his reply, she put the buckets on the porch and headed back inside.

Dawson finished the job as quickly as he could, though the stubborn goat made it more difficult. He wanted more time with Chloe before Tommy came home. There was still a lot he wanted to know. Like, was she involved with anyone? And, who else had she been with in the past nine years?

Okay, even to him, that last question was ridiculous, especially since he wouldn't want to share his history with her. By no means was he a man-whore, but as a rodeo cowboy, there had been a lot of women who appreciated his skills – in *and* out of the arena.

None had made him want to settle down, though. None had made him want to leave the rodeo world. It was a life he'd chosen as a way to earn enough to one day buy property – property like the Bartell Ranch. He'd used the money Hank had given him that fateful night so long ago to buy a horse, truck, and trailer. He was good – damn good – but the rodeo circuit was hard on relationships.

OVERDUE FOR LOVE | 89

It wasn't something he'd cared about before.

And I only care about it now because I have a son.

He finished milking just in time to see a late model Chevy pickup coming up the driveway. The horse and fancy lettering on the side gave the doctor's name and phone number, along with his credentials. Dawson hurried with the milk into the house, eager to see his son again, and to meet the man who'd brought him into the world.

Eager to size up his competition.

Chloe looked up. "I thought I heard Adam's truck."

"Yeah, I think he's here."

A second later, Tommy came tearing into the house, the screen door saved from slamming by a large hand. The good doctor entered, and Dawson's deepest desires *ahem* *misconceptions* were destroyed. The man before him was only a few years older than he was, with thick brown hair, warm golden eyes with crinkles around the corners, and not a hint of gray anywhere.

How could he *not* be Chloe's boyfriend? He was probably going to be popping the question next week. She was gorgeous and smart and self-sufficient and hardworking and Adam would be a real idiot not to have seen that for himself.

It took every ounce of self-control to shake Whitaker's hand and exchange pleasantries.

"Are you staying for dinner, Adam?" Chloe asked cheerfully.

Dawson chewed the inside of his cheek to shut himself up. He wasn't sure if he could live through a whole meal with Chloe's boyfriend. Chloe's handsome, young (well, at least not *old*), definitely not gay, veterinarian *boyfriend*.

Adam shook his head. "Already ate, thanks. You know Stetson's housekeeper, Carmelita — she can cook up a storm. She fed us as thanks for taking a look at Stet's cow."

"Oh good! How's their little one doing?"

Chloe seemed dead set on keeping Adam in the kitchen with them by engaging him in chitchat. It was obvious she was using Adam as a shield against having to deal with Dawson.

Well, Dawson didn't care. He could out-wait Adam any day of the week. He hip-checked the kitchen counter and smiled blandly at the two of them. He wasn't going anywhere.

"Growing like a sprout! I can hardly keep up with him."

"So I take it Tommy's eaten?"

Adam ruffled his hair. "Sure has, but you know this boy. I'm sure he could eat again."

Tommy shrugged. "I could eat." He, at least, did not seem obsessed with keeping the vet there. In fact, he seemed awfully anxious to go do something, shifting from foot to foot while trying to wait for his mom to dismiss him.

She's done a damn good job of raising a polite child.

After a surreptitious glance in Dawson's direction, the vet said, "Well, I'll leave you to it. It looks like a long night with Wildflower. Miss Lambert called on the way here."

"She's ready to foal?" Chloe's eyes sparkled. "We'll have to go visit her baby in a couple of days, huh, Tommy?" He nodded eagerly, finally interested in the topic. "In the meantime, I could bring you some dinner later, along with a thermos of soup or coffee."

With another sidelong glance at Dawson, Adam shook his head ruefully. "Thanks, but you've got company."

"Dawson *isn't* company," she said in a flat tone that made Dawson flinch.

Adam must've decided not to get into that discussion. "I'll see y'all later. Nice to meet you, Dawson." *Smart man.*

Dawson tipped his head, realizing he hadn't removed his hat. He took it off as the other man left the kitchen and headed out the back door.

"Go wash up," said Chloe to Tommy.

Still in the grips of jealousy even he realized he had no right to feel, he turned to Chloe as soon as their son clattered up the stairs. "Is that how you meet up with him? Take him soup late at night?" He scowled. "I guess it's better than screwing him in your bedroom. It must be close to Tommy's, since this house is so small. I appreciate your discretion in that, at least."

With a ruthless chop, Chloe split the head of iceberg lettuce in two before slamming the knife down on the counter. She stepped away from it as if trying to force herself to leave it alone. "How dare you?" she hissed at him, glaring daggers in his direction.

It was probably good she put the knife down on the counter.

"I don't want my son exposed to your affairs," he retorted defensively.

"My son considers Adam a friend, like I do. He's been a stand-in father, which is more than I can say for you, Mr. Sperm Donor. Whatever other relationship I have with him is *none* of your business."

She stepped back to the kitchen counter and began massacring the lettuce, chopping it into bits so fine, they'd be hard to spear with the tine of a fork.

Anger swelled in him. He had to admit, if only to himself, that he'd pushed her on this topic so hard because he'd expected her to deny the relationship, not leave the answer vague. "What kind of relationship do you have?" he demanded.

She licked her lips, her pink tongue darting out for just a moment, tantalizing him. "A cozy one."

She was officially trying to drive him crazy, and for the record, it was absolutely working.

CHAPTER 7

CHLOE

CHLOE KNEW SHE WAS playing with fire and shouldn't be taunting Dawson, but he was being such a jackass, she couldn't make herself care. She should be trying to keep Tommy from picking up on the anger between them. When he came downstairs, he'd feel it as soon as he walked into the room.

Woulda coulda shoulda.

"*Very* cozy," she repeated, poking the bear in the cage, chopping the lettuce like a maniac. It was so fine, it didn't even resemble lettuce any longer, but rather a mushy green slime.

Whatever. He could ask questions all day long, but he didn't deserve honesty, not after his accusations.

"Is it this kind?" He surged forward, hauling her into his arms to capture her mouth. She tried to twist away, but his arms held her immobile. His lips moved on hers, forcing her mouth to open so he could get his tongue inside. With a stifled moan, she melted against him, dropping the knife on the counter, hating herself even as she tangled her fingers in his black hair. Sensations she hadn't felt in nine years surged to life, leaving her aching for his touch.

He deepened the kiss, pulling her even closer. She lost count of the kisses and track of the time as their mouths worked in concert. A whimper of protest escaped her when he broke the kiss. He kissed along her jawline and cupped her breast. "This kind, Chloe? Does he touch you here?" She moaned when he palmed the sensitive flesh before circling his thumb around her nipple through the uniform top and sensible bra. Arching her back, she offered more silently, throwing her head back as he kissed her neck.

With one hand busy with her breast, the other one was suddenly at her thighs, pushing up the hem of her skirt while urging them apart. She began to obey when the thought of Tommy walking in on them jerked her back to reality, and she pulled away abruptly.

When he tried to pull her back, a growl in his throat, she held up her hand. "Stop. Tommy will be here in a moment." After a second, she could see he was visually revving down, though the bulge of his erection was obvious through his worn jeans.

With timing that usually only happened in the movies, she heard Tommy's footsteps clattering down the stairs and through the living room. Dawson's head jerked at the sound and then he said quietly, "We'll finish this later." She wasn't sure if it was a threat or a promise. Or a little of both.

She didn't reply as she busied herself with

finishing the minced salad. Dawson clearly expected to have sex with her. Why wouldn't he, after her shameful performance? She'd soaked him up like a sponge during a rainstorm in the desert. If Tommy hadn't been there, she would've done it. She damn well would've done it. A part of her wanted to send Tommy to Adam's house for the night so she could still do it.

It'd taken her several months to recover from a broken heart, three years to accept a date, and another three years before she'd consented to one awkward sex session with a guy that neither had wanted to repeat.

A few kisses and a couple of minutes with Dawson had undone all of her hard work.

As much as she despised Dawson and his treatment of her nine years ago, she still wanted him. What did that say about her? Was she a stereotypical sex-starved single mom? Chloe wouldn't have thought so a couple of days ago, before his return to her life. Now, she wanted to believe that. She *needed* to believe she craved contact so much that any man could elicit such a response.

Otherwise, that meant she still reacted like a wanton slut only with Dawson. She refused to believe that.

That just couldn't be true.

CHAPTER 8

CHLOE

*B*Y THE TIME Tommy was ready for bed, she was on tenterhooks. Since her son had asked Dawson to read him the next chapter in *Where the Red Fern Grows,* she didn't even have their nightly ritual to distract her from the dread consuming her.

Telling Dawson no was going to be unpleasant, to say the least. When he found out she wasn't going to sleep with him after their earlier encounter had worked him up, he might fly into a rage.

Actually, she realized as she thought about it, pacing around the kitchen, scrubbing everything in reach, she really had no idea how he would react. She just didn't know him well enough. She wished for the hundredth time that she'd had the common sense to realize she didn't know him very well nine years ago, *before* having sex with him.

Except…she shook her head. No, that really wasn't true. Despite the trouble it had caused her, and the loss of her father's emotional and financial support, she couldn't regret that night with Dawson. It had given her Tommy. That alone had made it worth it.

That night had also given her the most intense sexual experience of her life. She groaned, trying to smother the thought. Dwelling on how fantastic he'd been wasn't doing anything to strengthen her determination not to have a repeat performance.

Instead, she should focus on how angry she'd been when he'd mocked her virginity. His words, "A virgin who has no idea how to please a man," were burned into her brain with a branding iron. They'd echoed in her mind every time a cute guy gave her a smile at the grocery store. They'd echoed every time she'd thought about flirting with a customer at the restaurant. No one would want her. The only man she'd ever truly made love to had laughed at her afterwards.

It had messed with her mind, her self-esteem, her belief in her innate sexiness…it was almost difficult to state how much damage it had done. Only years of therapy and reading self-help books got her back to even being willing to smile at men again.

Quite frankly, it amazed her that he even *wanted* another go. He probably assumed she'd become more proficient in it over the years. Ha, that was a laugh. He'd just be disappointed all over again, and she'd end up rejected and destroyed again.

The sex *couldn't* be that good. It wasn't worth it.

She had coiled up into a chair to avoid sharing the couch with him, and she curled her hands into fists when she heard his footsteps approaching. He paused in the doorway, looking a little puzzled when he saw her in the chair. After a moment's hesitation, he walked toward her, crouching beside her instead of taking a seat on the oh-so-open-and-available couch. She curled her fists tighter.

"He's asleep."

Chloe nodded. "He was getting tired; he was blinking all through dinner."

"Is it always like that?" Dawson's eyes gleamed. "Does he always curl up with you to read and talk 'til he falls asleep?"

"Most of the time."

An expression she'd never seen crossed his face. "It's amazing. It makes me feel…" He trailed off before shrugging. "I don't know how to describe it."

Chloe nodded, reaching out to touch his shoulder without thought. "I know what you mean. I felt it the moment I first held him. It only gets stronger."

She pulled back, her hand flinching from his chest like she'd just touched a branding iron. *You can't touch him. You can't go down that path. No matter how sweet and kind he appears in this mo-*

ment, you know *what he is really like. You* know *he isn't to be trusted.*

He saw her pull back and frowned. "Are you okay?" he asked, reaching over to stroke her hair. She flinched.

"Let's just…let's just talk for a minute. I'll sit here and you can sit over there." She pointed at the couch. The *far* end of the couch. "And we'll talk all you want."

The corners of his mouth tightened and she could tell he was unhappy with where this was going, but he moved down to the far end of the couch and sat. The hurt in his eyes was like icepicks, taking chunks out of her heart, but Chloe couldn't let that get to her. She'd let him in one time, and only pain followed. She couldn't do it again.

"So," he said, obviously searching for a place to start, "how is Tommy doing in school?"

She grinned widely. Now *there* was a topic she could discuss all day long. She launched into his reading scores (off the charts) and his math scores (not as high) and his social skills (pretty good for an eight-year-old boy), and Dawson listened, his eyes intent on hers, smiling occasionally as she told proud-momma stories. She knew she was rambling at times, but it didn't seem like he minded.

This is his son we're discussing, not a stranger, even if they're really strangers to each other at the moment.

Her mind circled the idea of "at the moment" warily. That seemed to imply that in the future, they'd be more than that. And in all fairness to her son, they should be.

But still, it seemed…overwhelming. Scary. She wasn't ready to come to grips with that idea, not yet, so she shoved it away.

Finally, she ran out of Funny Tommy Stories to tell and decided it was time to change topics. Enough of her talking.

"How did you get into rodeoing?" she asked. "You didn't compete in them when you worked for my dad, did you? Or did I just not know?"

That idea seemed crazy to her – when he was working for her dad, there was very little she didn't know about him. She was, to put it kindly, obsessed with him.

Hormones have a way of doing that to you. That's all it was – hormones.

She just had to repeat that to herself about 62 more times and she might actually believe it.

"I did all through elementary school up to high school. That's where I learned to calf rope. There's not always a lot to do on reservations, but working with animals was something everyone seemed to encourage. For a long time, I borrowed the 4-H teacher's horse so I could take the Working Ranch Horse class and then after that, I got into the junior rodeo program, once I saved up enough money to buy my first horse."

Chloe shifted uncomfortably. She loved seeing the light in Dawson's eyes. She loved hearing him talk enthusiastically about working with animals. She loved learning things about him that she didn't know before.

And *that's* why she was uncomfortable. She didn't want to love anything about Dawson. Hate and anger were much easier to deal with. They didn't end with her heart being broken.

After a long silence, Dawson picked up his story again. "When your dad told me he'd changed his mind that night, he gave me all the money I'd been putting towards buying the Bartell Ranch, plus a couple thousand dollars extra to keep me quiet. Did he tell you that?"

Chloe shook her head mutely. To be honest, she hadn't really thought about it. She knew that her father had taken back his promise to sell the ranch to Dawson, but she hadn't thought much about it beyond that. His harsh words that night – *a virgin who has no idea how to please a man* – had rolled around in her head, blocking everything else out.

Everything until she'd looked at the pee stick and realized that her whole life was about to change.

But no, she hadn't spent much time thinking about how that night had affected Dawson, too. She felt a little guilt flush through her.

Just a little.

"I used that money to get my start in the rodeo world. It's not cheap to ride the rodeo circuit – there's entry fees and gas and hotel rooms and restaurant costs. I wouldn't have been able to do it without the check your father handed me that night. It was my hush money, and I was a good boy. I hushed right up."

The silence that descended over the room then was stifling. The tick of the clock on the wall seemed as loud as her heartbeat. What was she going to do? Who was this man? She thought she'd fallen in love with him all those years ago, but it had been lust. Now, she was left in the bizarre predicament of sharing a child with a stranger.

He scooted to the other end of the couch so he could reach for her. She instinctively drew back. She wasn't ready for that, not by a long shot.

"Not now," she said. *Not ever*, her mind said.

She ignored that thought. Too much to decide right now. She could think about it later.

Dawson nodded his head, and even if he wasn't happy – the tight corners of his mouth had reappeared – he at least seemed to be understanding.

"Tomorrow is the first day of the rodeo," he said. "I know that Tommy would love to come with me and hang out with all the horses in the paddocks. I'll pay for his ticket to get in so you don't have to. I think he has horse fever as much as I did when I was a kid."

Chloe's mouth quirked at that. Yeah, that was the understatement of the century. She'd never really understood the fascination with horses – they were so big and tall, they were scary and intimidating to her – but Tommy got bit by horse fever since he was old enough to know what a horse was. She'd always assumed that had come from her father, but it seemed like it was, yet again, something else that had come from Dawson.

Tommy really was a "mini me" of Dawson.

"He would enjoy that," she said slowly. It scared the living daylights out of her to allow Tommy to spend time with Dawson like that without her around, but on the other hand, they were father and son. Tommy should get to know his father. Dawson should get to know his son.

No matter how much that scared her.

With one last look that said so much without him saying a word, he headed out the front door and over to the Drop-Inn Motel. Chloe collapsed against the chair and squeezed her eyes tight.

I did the right thing. I did.

I did.

So why do I feel like shit?

CHAPTER 9

DAWSON

*A*FTER A SLEEPLESS NIGHT ON A BED made out of what he'd swear was plywood and rocks, Dawson headed over to the house bright and early. He was never one to sleep in much, but with the promise of being able to spend the day with Tommy and Chloe, he couldn't fathom sleeping another moment.

You're only spending the day with Tommy. Don't get your hopes up for something more than that.

He turned down the long, dirt road, the bumps in the road as jarring as his thoughts. The sun was peeking over the horizon, sending long beams of golden light into the sky, almost as if nature was welcoming him to Chloe's place.

Not her place — the vet's place. Don't forget that. For all you know, they're dating. And if yesterday was anything to judge by, you're not going to find out the truth about that relationship for quite some time, if ever.

His gut tightened at the thought. He grimly wished for his gay, wizened old vet that he'd imagined in his mind when Chloe had been describing him. If only…

He pulled into the circular driveway and cut the engine. The morning sounds surrounded him — birds chirping, cows lowing to each other, and yup, there was the goat. Her high-pitched bleating were a good reminder that he needed to get to milking. Anything that saved Chloe time and energy were good for him to do.

The *neighborly* thing to do.

On the front porch, he hesitated. Yesterday, Tommy had been up and awake, and Dawson had entered the house with his permission. Just entering this morning without anyone's permission seemed a bit…questionable. But on the other hand, knocking loudly and forcing Chloe to wake up and let him in did seem to defeat the purpose.

He finally knocked quietly to assuage his conscience, then tried the doorknob. Yup, unlocked. He should talk to Chloe about locking up at night. Living out in the country without any protection was a dangerous thing to do.

Except, she probably wouldn't want to hear a word about it. He wasn't her father or her lover, and he needed to stop acting like it.

He tiptoed through the living room as best he could in his cowboy boots, and then up to the second floor. He looked down the hallway and saw Chloe's door was partially open. God, he was so damn tempted to sneak down there and just peek in. She'd never even know, and then he could find out what kind of nightgown she slept in…or none at all.

His groin tightened at the thought, but he pushed it all away. He couldn't, just *could not*, do that. No matter how much he wanted to.

He instead pushed the door open to his son's room – *oh, what a thought!* – and saw him sleeping peacefully in bed, his arm flung wide. His PJs, covered in cowboy hats, went right along with his bedspread, covered in horseshoes.

Yup, definitely my kid.

He tiptoed over and gently shook Tommy awake.

"Whaaa…oh hi Dawson!" Tommy exclaimed, shooting straight up in bed, a huge grin on his face.

Dawson grinned back. "Good morning," he whispered. "I want to surprise your mom again – what do you think about helping me with the morning chores?"

"Do I get to put my hand under the chickens and steal their eggs again?!" Tommy asked in as hushed-as-an-eight-year-old boy's voice ever got.

"Sure." Dawson tried to keep the laughter out of his voice, but he had to admit that he failed spectacularly on that front.

Tommy sprang out of bed and whipped on a sweatshirt over his PJs and slipped his cowboy boots onto his bare feet.

"No socks?" Dawson asked, eyebrow cocked. Tommy just shrugged, so Dawson let it go. If he wasn't worried, Dawson wouldn't be either.

Hand-in-hand, they snuck back down the stairs and out the back door, snagging the milk buckets on the way.

"So how come your mom doesn't let you do the chores with her every morning?" Dawson asked as they headed for the chicken coop.

Tommy shrugged again. "She does, she just doesn't let me steal the eggs or milk the goat," he clarified. "If there's no chicken on the nest, she lets me take the eggs, but she doesn't want me pecked at, so no egg stealing. And she won't let me into the stalls with the animals."

Dawson's mouth tightened and he simply nodded in response to Tommy's answer. It wouldn't do to make his first act as fatherhood be, "Question all decisions made by Chloe thus far," but he really wanted to have a chat with her some time soon. If she kept this up, Tommy would be a teenager and would have no idea how to work. You have to start kids young. If they're raised to be afraid of animals, or at least not comfortable with them, it made it harder to teach them respect for the animals later on.

After some pointers on egg gathering to keep flapping wings and squawking to a minimum, they then headed to the barn. Closing the door on the chicken coop behind them, Dawson made a mental note to fix the broken hinge. Even if Chloe had the mechanical skills to do it, which he wasn't sure she did, she probably didn't have the time or the tools.

In fact, looking around the barn and the farm as a whole, he could see areas of neglect. The vet was probably busy with his mom and his career, and Chloe certainly had enough on her hands. Running a farm was no mean feat, and Dawson was surprised she'd held on as long as she had.

They practiced milking once again, and Tommy showed a little improvement over the day before. Day by day, he'd get better, until he was an old hand at it like Dawson.

Wet lips touched his back the same time that his shirt got yanked out of his jeans.

"What the hell?" he exclaimed, whipping around and coming face to face with Ivy, who'd managed to stick her head sideways through the slats in the stall and reach his shirt. She had her teeth wrapped around the fabric and just kept pulling it further into her mouth. Tommy was absolutely *no* help at all, doubled over with laughter as he was.

Dawson narrowed his eyes at his son for a moment and then the humor of the situation hit him and he grinned at Tommy.

"Is there *anything* Ivy won't eat?" he asked him dryly as he wrestled to get his shirt out of the goat's mouth. Ivy clamped down further, chewing as she went, slobber flying everywhere. Finally, Dawson smacked Ivy on the nose, startling her into letting go. He looked down at his shirt, a mangled mess, and grimaced. He'd definitely have to stop by the Drop-Inn Motel on the way over to the rodeo. He couldn't show up looking like *this*.

Tommy just grinned. "Not anything I've

found," he said cheerfully. "We caught her eating ivy one time, which is when Mom renamed her."

"Oh? What was she called before that?"

"Dumbass," Tommy said with a shrug.

Dawson tried not to choke on his laughter, but really, it was close.

"Adam named her," Tommy continued. "Mom said Ivy was a better name."

"I'm sure she did," Dawson murmured under his breath.

Pails of milk and eggs in hand, they headed back to the house.

"So your mom said I can take you to the rodeo with me today."

"*Really?!*" Tommy squealed happily. "Yay! Does this mean I can ride your horse? Can I pet him? I could brush him and do a real good job, I promise!"

"I'm sure you would," Dawson said. *Especially after I teach you how.* "We'll be able to do all of that and more."

"Yaaaahhhhhoooooooo!"   Tommy

whooped, and went running into the house, letting the screen door slam behind him.

Yet another thing to teach him to do properly.

There were so many things about becoming a man that Dawson wanted to teach Tommy. He didn't want to leave after this weekend and pretend he never met him. Every moment that he spent with Tommy, Dawson fell in love with him just a little more.

Was he ready to be a dad?

Only one way to find out…

CHAPTER 10

DAWSON

*T*HE WARM SUMMER SUN beat down on his head and shoulders, and he wiped his forehead with the back of his arm. Damn, even up here in the mountains of Idaho, summers got a little warm to be standing around in direct sunlight.

"Dawson," Tommy said, "look at this one! It's got *spots!*" He pointed at a paint horse that was contentedly chewing on a mouthful of hay, completely ignoring Tommy's yelling.

That was good, at least. Most horses didn't appreciate the kind of noise Tommy seemed to love to make.

Dawson ambled over and they admired and petted the horse, while Tommy told Dawson all about how he wanted to ride horses all the time, but he only got to when Adam had time for it and Adam didn't very often and he'd told his mom that having a horse would help out around the farm but she never seemed to believe him and he didn't understand why, because of *course* having horses could only help and—

"Do you want something to eat for lunch?" Dawson cut in, finally realizing that if he was going to wait for his son to stop talking on his own volition, they could both starve to death long before that.

"Oh yeah!" Tommy said and jumped off the railing of the corral, heading towards the food stalls. Dawson's stomach rumbled, and he had to remind himself that he didn't want to stuff himself too full. Nothing like jumping off a horse and sprinting towards a calf with an overfilled belly that jiggled with every step. He'd made that mistake before and had ended that event by upchucking behind the calf corral.

No siree bob, he did not gorge on fair food any longer, no matter how good the fry bread smelled.

After buying Slurpees, fry bread, corndogs, french fries, and a turkey leg, they made their way over to a shady spot underneath a tree. As they sat down in the dappled shade, Dawson closed his eyes with a happy sigh. Damn, that felt nice.

He opened his eyes and began digging into their feast with his son, laughing as they talked, but trying to casually watch him eat. The way Tommy grinned up at Dawson...it was his smile. It was his face looking up at him. The same face he'd seen in the mirror his whole childhood.

It was a little creepy, and a whole lot amazing, to see that. How had he just not *known* in some deep part of his soul that his son existed? How had he not just sensed it?

"So you're my daddy, aren't you?" Tommy

asked, munching away on the fry bread covered with a sprinkle of cinnamon and sugar.

"I…uh…" Dawson stuttered. He hadn't exactly asked Chloe if it was okay if he discuss this topic with Tommy, and he was suddenly completely unsure what Chloe would want him to say. Surely she wouldn't want him to lie to their son, right? Sending up a quick prayer for forgiveness for what he was about to do, Dawson nodded slowly.

"Yeah, I'm your daddy," he said, and the love that ran through him at those words took his breath away. It was so damn amazing to say those words to someone he didn't even know just days ago.

"How did you find us?" Tommy asked. "Did you search for Mom and me through Google?"

"No, I didn't know to look for you. I was just stopping at Betty's to eat lunch and there was your momma. I was so surprised, you coulda knocked me over with a feather. And then when I was leaving, you came walking through the door. Do you remember – you almost ran me over."

"I did?" Tommy asked, eyes round with surprise.

"Yeah, you came barreling through that door, running for your mom. Didn't even notice me. But as soon as I saw you, I knew you were mine."

Tommy got real quiet, shoving and chewing, shoving and chewing french fries into his mouth as he thought. Once he swallowed it all down with a gulp of Slurpee, he asked, "Why didn't you look for me before?" His voice was quiet, and the pain was thick.

Dawson's heart hurt.

"I didn't know. If I'd known…Tommy, I would've been here. Every step of the way, I would've been here. What…what has your mom told you?" At least if he knew Chloe's story, he could try to keep his in line with hers. She might already want to kill him just for saying what he has, but Dawson couldn't let Tommy keep thinking that he hadn't wanted him. The very idea made his soul ache.

"She told me that she was in love with my daddy – that's you – and then you guys had to split apart because of my grandpa. She won't let me see him, even though she says that he has a giant horse farm down in Arizona. Do you know my grandpa? Does he have a lot of horses?"

This, at least, was safer ground. He could discuss Hank Bartell without bringing up his personal relationship with Chloe, or a lack thereof. She sure as shit didn't want Tommy knowing that he was the result of one night of passion and hatred, and nothing more.

"I worked for your grandpa for a long time," Dawson said quietly. He didn't want to talk up the man, but he also didn't want to bad-mouth him. "He does own a lot of horses – one of the top breeding programs in the country, actually. I never could figure out how your momma came from your grandpa. Your mom doesn't care one lick about horses."

"I know," Tommy said sadly. The look on his face was nothing short of heartbreaking.

Dawson remembered what it was like to want a horse so bad, his teeth ached.

"What does your mom tell you about your grandpa?" Dawson asked, curious.

"Just that he wasn't real happy with her about me, but that she loves me anyway and that's all that matters. That my grandpa has a lot of horses. That he lives in the desert where it's really hot all the time. Do I have a grandma?"

"No, sorry. She died giving birth to your momma," Dawson said quietly.

"Darn. I like to think that I had a grandma out there who wants to make me all the cookies I can eat."

"I think that'd be a lot of cookies," Dawson said with a grin and a wink. It felt good to smile about something, and get back to safer ground.

"Lots and lots of cookies!" Tommy said, grinning back. "I only love cotton candy more than I love cookies." He looked, not so subtly, towards the cotton candy booth just two stalls down from their shady retreat. Dawson laughed. The sheer conniving of his son was a *sure* sign he was Dawson's. He spent most of his own childhood trying to convince his grand-mother to give him "just one more cookie."

"Well, it isn't a rodeo unless you're eating cotton candy," Dawson said, mock seriously. They gathered up their trash and threw it away on the way to the cotton candy booth. After picking out the biggest one he could find and Dawson paying for it, Tommy tore into the sugary cloud, grinning ecstatically as he did.

Oh yeah, he was Dawson's son all right.

CHAPTER 11

CHLOE

TOMMY BOUNCED on the wooden bench next to Chloe as Kurtis Workman, the person who did practically all of the announcing for public events in the area, started in again. "Coming up next is Dawson Blackhorse, a calf roper riding his horse Bolt. They've been climbing up the ranks for the last couple of years. Let's see how he does against our hometown roper, Dave Smithers, here in the Sawyer Stampede."

With that, the gate on one side of the arena flew open, allowing the calf to run in, as Dawson came tearing out of the other side. It was just moments and the lasso was flying through the air, wrapping around the calf's feet.

"Yeaaaaahhhhhhhhh!" Tommy was on his feet, crowing with excitement as his dad threw himself off his horse and onto the ground, wrapping the rope around three of the calf's feet and jerking clear. It was all over in just seconds and Chloe realized with a huff that she could start breathing again. She shouldn't care if Dawson did well, truly, but it was hard not to whoop and holler along with her son.

As the crowd died down, the Kurtis' voice came back. "A smokin' hot 14.87 seconds! That easily puts Dawson Blackhorse in first place. Let's see if he can keep that speed tomorrow night, when he enters the arena again."

Dawson and Bolt trotted out of the ring, the calf scampering out the other way, and the next calf and rider were let into the ring to the roar of the crowd.

"Mom?" Tommy croaked. Chloe looked over to find her son looking a little...green?

"Mom, I don't feel so good."

Oh God. She jumped to her feet and grabbed Tommy's hand, heading for the exit from the bleachers. "Let's go," she urged him, tugging his arm a little harder when he slowed down for a moment.

"Mom?" he said. "I really, really don't feel good." She glanced over and saw that he'd turned a nice pea green color. *Oh Lordy.* She scooped him up in her arms and ran faster. She just needed to get him to a patch of grass or a trash can or at least not in the stands of the arena—

Bleeecccccchhhhhh...

He retched in her arms, all down her shirt, her shoulder, down her back, and into her hair.

"Eewwww..." a little girl squealed who'd been walking by.

Tell me about it.

Chloe didn't stop to find out if the girl'd been in the hit zone when Tommy had vomited or not. Let her parents take care of her. She had own little boy to take care of.

And a shower to take.

Her own stomach started to rebel as the

stench of the throw up hit her nostrils. She'd always been a sympathy puker, and really, having her clothes covered in it was *not* helping the situation.

She made it out to the parking lot and gingerly slid Tommy into the backseat. "We're gonna get you home," she said, stroking the hair away from his forehead. "It's gonna be fine."

She hurried around to the driver's side, holding her breath and refusing to look down as she scurried. She was *not* going to throw up, she was *not* going to throw up…

"How long have you not felt good, baby?" she asked, throwing the car in gear and peeling out of the parking lot. She rolled the windows down, trying to keep the stench from overwhelming her.

"Just for a couple of minutes," Tommy said miserably. "I didn't know I was gonna throw up. I'm sorry, Mommy." He so rarely called her that; it made her heart twist with equal parts pain and love when she heard it. She punched the gas, pressing the pedal to the floorboards.

"What did you eat today?" she asked. Maybe one of the booths was selling rotten food. She'd have to tell Dawson to keep an ear out for other cases of food poisoning.

"A Slurpee and an ice cream cone and a fried Twinkie and a corn dog and a hamburger and fry bread and two sticks of cotton candy and kettle corn and a pickle. Oh, and french fries."

She almost swerved off the road and into the ditch. "You ate all of that *today*?" she screeched. She knew she should keep calm and not yell, but there was only so much a body could take.

"Yeah, Dawson bought it for me. Why?"

"Why?!" she echoed, exasperated. "Because that's enough to kill off a grown man! You do *not* need to eat that much sugar! Or, that much food!"

"Oh." He was quiet for a minute. "So if I eat too much, I get sick?"

They were bouncing erratically along the rutted dirt driveway and Chloe slowed down, just a smidge. She couldn't handle the smell much longer but having her stomach jiggled that much wasn't helping things, either.

"Yeah. That's why I don't let you eat everything in sight." She wasn't sure if she should laugh or cry. Had Dawson *never* taken care of a small child before?!

"Oh," he said again. He was quiet the rest of the way down the driveway. She wondered if and for how long this lesson would stick. Her child was the king of junk food, and she'd fought with him for eight long years over how much crap he should be able to shove in his mouth. When they finally got to the house – which only *seemed* like an eternity and a half – she made sure to leave the windows rolled all the way down when she parked the car. The last thing she wanted to do was trap *that* smell inside of it.

After cleaning him up and giving him a dose of the bright pink nausea medicine, she tucked him into bed and then climbed into the shower herself. She firmly closed her eyes as the hot water washed over her, refusing to look at the food chunks as they swirled down the drain.

I think I'm gonna make Dawson and Tommy clean the car tomorrow morning. Maybe then they'll learn something from this.

And then she headed to bed at the ungodly early hour of 8:30. Being puked on in public did tend to wear a body out.

CHAPTER 12

CHLOE

*S*HE AWOKE with her nose twitching.
Is that…bacon?

Her eyes popped open and she looked toward the bedroom window. The light was barely beginning to steal through the lace curtains. It had to be stupidly early.

She swung her legs over the side of the bed and with a big yawn, brought her old-fashioned alarm clock — complete with two little bells on top — close to her face so she could read the time.

5:30 in the morning? Why was there bacon cooking in her house at 5:30 in the morning?

Or, at all, really?

It had to be Dawson. No thief broke into a house just to cook her breakfast, and Tommy wouldn't get up at 5:30 in the morning to cook for her, either.

She yawned again and shuffled off the bed and toward her slippers. Despite her (in her opinion) well-deserved anger towards Dawson over the Food Incident of 2017, and the fact that he apparently just stole into her house this morning without asking permission before-hand, she couldn't find it in herself to actually be upset with him.

She *should* be but somehow, she wasn't.

Any man who broke into her house to cook bacon and – nose twitching – coffee was a-okay in her book.

She shuffled her way down the stairs, and to the kitchen. Yup, there was Dawson, a kitchen towel slung over his shoulder, whistling a tuneless song as he cooked. He looked over and his face lit up.

"Good morning!" he said cheerfully. "Coffee's ready." He jerked his head towards the coffee maker that was bubbling and spurting its way through a fresh pot. She wandered over, pouring herself a cup, and then wandered back to the kitchen doorway, leaning against it as she watched him work. The silence between them was easy and she found herself smiling.

"So, where'd the bacon come from?" she finally asked, as he laid strips of golden brown out on a plate and added fresh strips to the pan.

"The Shop 'N Go." He flashed her a grin. "I haven't been here long enough to build a pig pen and raise my own pigs, at least not yet."

She rolled her eyes playfully, even as her heart caught on the words *not yet*. Did that mean in the future…?

"I asked Tommy what his favorite breakfast was, and he told me bacon and Mickey Mouse pancakes, and then very sadly told me that you guys don't eat bacon very often. So I figured that it was safe to assume you didn't have any in the fridge. I stopped at the Shop 'N Go after the rodeo ended last night." He opened the oven door and slipped the plate in with the cooked bacon.

She looked at the temperature dial – it was set on the lowest heat level allowable. She glanced at him, startled, and he shrugged. "I couldn't afford a housekeeper, so I had to teach myself how to cook. Number one rule of food: Keep cold food cold, and hot food hot. Things taste better that way. Why don't you sit down at the dining room table?" He nodded to the open doorway that led out into the dining room.

She shook her head. She didn't want to be that far away from him as he weaved his magic. It was too much fun watching him work.

"I have a confession to make," he said, staring at the frying pan as the bacon cooked. He wasn't meeting her gaze, which made the hair on the back of her neck prickle.

"Yeah?" she said lightly, trying to pretend as if he wasn't scaring her.

"I told Tommy I was his dad yesterday. At the rodeo. I didn't know what you wanted me to tell him, but he was asking questions and…I didn't want to start our relationship out by bald-faced lying to him. He needs to know that he can trust me to tell him the truth, no matter what. I already have a lot of ground to make up with him. You know?" He finally tore his gaze away from the popping bacon and stared her in the eye. "If you want to rip me a new one, I understand. It was a big decision for me to make on my own."

She thought back to her own cowardly avoidance of the topic when Tommy had asked her, and she knew that Dawson's way was better. Tommy deserved to know the truth.

"You were right to do it. I should've told him that first night you walked into the diner, but I'd kept hoping you'd just keep on walking and not come back." She gave a low, humorless chuckle. "Anyway, Tommy should get to know you as his dad, not just as a random stranger off the street. To be honest, I think he was probably already sure of the answer, and just wanted someone to confirm his suspicions. He asked me the same question and I ducked it, 'cause I'm a coward."

He smiled gently at her. "Never a coward. You've lived through things that would kill off a lesser woman."

She settled back against the door jam, smiling as she sipped at her coffee again. What a way to start a Saturday morning, even if it was still stupidly early. This was worth it.

"Oh!" she gasped, suddenly remembering. "Tommy and food! You and I need to have a talk about that."

She stopped and thought for a moment, trying to think of the best way to say it. She really didn't know how to discuss the topic tactfully, so with a mental shrug of the shoulders, she just dove in. "You can't just feed Tommy everything he wants. He puked all over me last night."

Dawson froze, hand mid-air as he was whipping the pancake batter. "What?" he breathed, dark eyes wide.

"Yeah. All that junk food you fed him — enough to get a grown man sick? Well, guess what it does to an eight-year-old's stomach?" she asked dryly. "After we watched you ride, he started to get sick. He was so excited about watching you ride, he'd begun bouncing up and down on the bench and I think that was just about the last straw for his poor intestines."

The corners of Dawson's mouth quirked up and she could tell he was fighting back laughter. She narrowed her eyes at him and glared. "Sooooo…" she said slowly, "next time you want to be a dad to Tommy, you need to do things like *not* say yes to every request he makes."

He sobered up. "Yeah, I know. I'm sorry. I shouldn't have. We were just talking about your mom and dad and he was making sad faces and then…I was saying yes to everything. I shouldn't have. It was…easier than saying no."

"Well, as punishment for you *both*, you two get to clean every last bit of puke out of my car," Chloe said sternly. "Maybe that'll inspire him to ask less often and for you to say no more often."

Dawson grimaced but nodded as he poured

the pancake batter into the frying pan, sizzling and popping as it hit the hot surface. "Fair enough," he said. "Oh, I don't know what your plans are for today, but I wanted to take you two to the rodeo and fair. While there, I could feed our amazing son," Chloe's heart clenched at the word *our,* "seven bags of cotton candy and then put him on the Tilt-O-Whirl. I mean, he should learn to toughen up, and not just up-chuck at the slightest provocation. He really needs to stop being such a pansy."

Chloe, who'd started out thinking he was being serious, was laughing by time he was done. She snagged the towel from his shoulder and began beating him over the head and shoulders with it.

"You," *whack,* "sir," *whack,* "are no," *whack,* "help!" He grabbed the end of the towel, and wrapping it around his fist, began drawing her closer, his eyes dropping to her lips as he reeled her in.

"I have lots of ideas," he breathed quietly, staring down at her, eyes alight. "Maybe some of the other ones would be helpful."

The grin faded from her face as she stared up at him, her breath caught in her throat. She wanted so badly to go up on her tiptoes and press her lips against his and…

She backed away, dropping her hand from the kitchen towel. "I think I'll have to pass," she said lightly, forcing levity into her voice, trying to keep it from shaking as she did. *Casual. You're so casual.* "I can go with you guys to the fair for a little while, but I need to go grocery shopping today, as you already noticed. That's going to require a trip to Boise. I don't make enough money to shop regularly at the Shop 'N Go – they're just stupidly expensive, something else I'm sure you noticed. Usually, I drag Tommy along with me to Boise but I'm sure he'd much rather stay with you at the rodeo instead. Oh, and I also have to go into work in a little bit and cover the morning rush. With the Sawyer Stampede in town, Betty's is going to be filled to the brim."

Before Dawson could answer, Tommy shuffled into the kitchen, his midnight hair sticking up wildly in every direction. "Hey Mom, hey

Dawson," he said around a yawn and then collapsed at the kitchen table, putting his head down on his arms as he did so. "Smells yummy, Dawson," he mumbled, not even bothering to open his eyes.

"How you feeling this morning?" Dawson asked, flipping a pancake over, then pulling a jug of orange juice out of the fridge.

Yet something else he must've brought home from the Shop 'N Go. That gallon of OJ probably put him back $7. *Oh, to be that rich…*

"Better," he mumbled, his eyes still closed. "I threw up all over Mom yesterday."

"Yeah, I heard," Dawson said. "And as punishment, you and I get to clean your mom's car, *before* she drives to Boise in it. So why don't you eat up real fast so we can put your mom's car to rights while she's taking a shower?" He slid a plate with bacon and Mickey Mouse pancakes in front of Tommy, along with a glass of orange juice. He poured…was that real maple syrup? It was in a glass bottle. *I haven't bought real maple syrup in…well, ever. I forgot what it's like to be rich!*

Tommy shot straight up, his eyes glowing with happiness.

"You remembered!" he crowed, digging into the pancakes excitedly.

"It was just yesterday," Dawson said dryly, but winked at Tommy who grinned back, his mouth full of pancake and syrup.

"Tommy!" Chloe said, trying to stifle her groan at the sight. "Not with your mouth full!"

He opened up his mouth, thought better of it, chewed, swallowed and then said, "Sorry, Mom." She stroked his hair off his forehead, trying to get his cowlick to behave for once. He looked like a Native American version of Calvin from *Calvin and Hobbes* at the moment, and she couldn't help grinning at him. He was just too damn adorable most days.

Especially the days where he didn't puke on her.

Dawson slid a plate in front of Chloe, also loaded down with food, and said, "Eat up! You need to get some fat on your bones. I'm afraid you're going to blow away any moment now."

She ignored that comment but dug into her

pancakes lustily anyway. If she was going to get fat, homemade pancakes with real maple syrup was the way to do it.

CHAPTER 13

DAWSON

*D*AWSON JUMPED OFF BOLT and rubbed him down, taking off his saddle and halter before giving him a small sugar cube that he ate eagerly. "Good boy," he crooned in his horse's ear as he curried the sweat and straw out of Bolt's mane. "You've been doing so good," he told him. Bolt's ear flickered. He may not understand what Dawson was saying, but he did understand that tone of voice.

While Dawson cleaned up his horse for the day – yet another first place win for Bolt and him – he wondered eagerly if Chloe and Tommy were going to be there that night. He'd asked Chloe to stay after the calf roping event was done, but she'd just shrugged and told him she'd think about it. He wanted to know; the suspense was starting to get to him.

Finally done with cleanup, he led Bolt to a horse stall in the Long Valley County Barn, a place he could rent out for Bolt during the rodeo. Some people kept their horses in the horse trailer the whole time, saving on fees, but Dawson never did. He wanted to treat his best friend and working buddy the absolute best way possible. With a final pat to his neck, Dawson headed back out in search of Chloe and Tommy. Her bright blonde hair contrasting against his pitch-black hair shouldn't be hard to spot, right? Dawson searched through the crowds milling about, the sidewalks between vendors full of couples and families out for an evening together.

Had she left after all? Had Tommy gotten sick again? Dawson had only given in to Tommy's pleadings once and had let him eat one ball of cotton candy. But surely that didn't make him sick. Maybe she just didn't want to be around Dawson. Maybe, despite how warm and open she'd seemed that morning, she was second guessing her choice to have him in her life again. Maybe—

The flash of platinum blonde hair caught his eye and he spun towards the sight, spotting the top of her head through the crowds. Hurriedly, he wove his way past slower pedestrians, suddenly anxious to get to her. He wanted to see her face, wanted to see Tommy's face, wanted…

Except, she was alone. He glanced around, looking for Tommy – maybe he'd wandered over to look at a vendor's booth – but Chloe's voice cut through the noise around them. "He's still not feeling good," Chloe said. "I dropped him off at Adam and Ruby's house for the night. I appreciate you only giving him one ball of cotton candy today, but I think it was still a little much for an already sensitive stomach."

Dawson had finally gotten to her and, picking up her hands, stared down at her. God, she was so damn beautiful. He wondered for a moment if she even realized how much it hurt – in the best way possible – to see her smile at him. Something he'd never expected to see again.

"Sorry. I thought I was being good by only giving him one wand of it. His soulful brown eyes staring up at me? He's damn hard to resist."

Much like his mother, except his eyes are brown instead of a rich green.

"Oh, I've noticed," she replied dryly, the edges of her eyes crinkling in amusement. "He's been plying his wares on me for eight years. I've just grown a thicker skin."

They began wandering through the booths then, hand in hand, the smell of fair food and bull poop mixing together to create a rich aroma that can only be found at county fairs.

It was a smell he adored.

"So, did you see my win?" he asked a little too casually. She nodded. "Just one more day and the Sawyer Stampede is over. But do you know what a winning cowboy likes to do to celebrate their wins?" He pulled them to a stop and gathered her against him, nestling her between his thighs.

She shook her head and then said hesitantly, "Dawson, I don't know if I'm—"

"They like to take their favorite girl out dancing," he broke in. "You ready to do some Boot Scootin' Boogie-ing with me?"

She laughed, the concern and hesitation gone. "Yes, I'd love it!" she said happily.

He grabbed her hand, soft and slim in his roughened bear paws, and began pulling her towards the large grassy area where music had begun thumping already. He'd thought she'd love it – she may not have been into horses growing up, but she did years of dance. The times he'd seen her in tights…well, the memories still made him break out into a sweat.

They joined a line dance, and once…did she *mean* to swing her hip and bump his? He glanced over and her eyes, lit up and green and brilliant, gave him his answer.

Dawson Blackhorse, Ms. Chloe Bartell is flirting with you. Don't hesitate – seize the moment!

So as the line began moving the other direction, he did a hipcheck on her. She grinned up at him, and her tongue flicked out over her pink, rosy lips.

He felt his groin tighten in response. Oh man, she was delicious. He had visions of that amazing mouth going down on him and he closed his eyes for just a moment, breathing in through his nose, out through his mouth. He *had* to keep himself under control. At least in public.

The live band switched over to *The Dance* by Garth Brooks, and all thoughts of keeping himself under control were swept away as Dawson roughly pulled Chloe into his arms. He wanted – no, *needed* – her there. Against him. He pulled her against his body and they swayed to the music, listening as the haunting lyrics rang out.

The song finally ended, and Dawson reluctantly stepped back. It was hard to drop his arms, to not be holding Chloe against him and he hesitated for a moment. Maybe he could –

"Hey Dawson!" someone said, slapping him on the shoulder. Dawson swallowed hard and turned to see Rex, a bull rider and someone who he usually loved to see, standing there. "You're killing it in the rankings right now. I can't wait to see how you do tomorrow! Are you going to the Northern Rodeo Association Finals in Billings after this?"

Without even looking, he felt Chloe stiffen and then move away.

Dammit, this is what I get for not talking to her before now. Dawson could've cursed a blue streak in frustration, but bit down on his tongue instead.

"No," he told Rex. "I have a kid here, turns out, and so I'll be here for the long run. I don't know if I'll continue the rodeo circuit or not, but I'm not going anywhere, not for a long time."

Rex's eyes flicked towards Chloe's stiff back as she chatted with some other dance attendees, attempting to smile as she talked to them. Even from here, Dawson could see it was forced, and his gut twisted.

"A kid, huh?" Rex said, the surprise evident on his face. He paused for just a second, his eyes flicking back and forth between Dawson and Chloe. "Well, I see…" Rex said slowly, and winked at Dawson. "I'm going to head down to O'Malley's and get a bite to eat, but I'll see you around. Wish you all the best," he said, jerking his head towards Chloe, and then disappeared into the crowd, his white cowboy hat quickly swallowed up by the hundreds just like it.

Dawson headed towards Chloe, his fists clenching and then releasing as he walked. He was *not* going to let a little misunderstanding come between them, not after all they've been through already.

He slipped his arm around Chloe's waist, which caused her to stiffen even further. "Let's dance," he whispered in her ear. The band had obligingly switched back to a slow song, so he was able to pull Chloe away from her discussion with the gaggle of women and back to the dance floor, which in this case was just a giant swath of grass.

At least he didn't have to try to talk to her while doing the Macarena. Small blessings.

He pulled her into his arms and unlike last

time, where she'd been pliable as putty, this time she was unbending, as rigid and cold as a bar of steel.

"Rex is an old rodeo friend," he said, figuring that facts were always a good place to start. "He doesn't know that I've been thinking of maybe staying here for a little while." Instead of softening her up, this just seemed to make her more stiff. Not exactly his intended effect. "I don't want to leave, Chloe. Not right now. Not when I'm just starting to get to know my son." He stopped swaying and lifted her chin to meet his eyes. People continued dancing around him but neither of them noticed. They were in their own world, their own universe, as they stood there.

"I don't know where this is going between you and I, or if it's even going anywhere. What I do know is that I'm not ready to walk away from you or Tommy. Give us some time."

She softened a little – just a smidge. But it happened. He smiled, feeling victorious. It was amazing what a little looseness, a little relaxation of the mouth, could do for his soul.

"For right now, let's just be us. Let's dance."

She nodded and lifted her arms, draping them around his neck. He pulled her close, and as the music flowed around them, they swayed and laughed and fell just a little bit in love.

CHAPTER 14

DAWSON

THEY TUMBLED THROUGH THE FRONT DOOR, Chloe shushing Dawson as they went. "You're going to wake up Tommy," she whispered loudly.

He couldn't hold back his laugh, he really couldn't. It was a real treat to see Chloe drunk. Between dances, he got her soused on wine coolers, an increasingly entertaining state of being for her.

"Chloe, you dropped Tommy off at Adam's house, remember? I gave him cotton candy so he wasn't feeling good...?"

"Oh!" she said, her eyes rounded in surprise. "I forgot about that. I can't believe I forgot that. How did I do that?"

"A lot of wine coolers," he said dryly.

"Huh."

Which seemed to be all she had to say on the topic, which was fine by him. He wanted her in bed, and that meant less talking and more walking.

He grabbed her hand and began pulling her up the stairs. "I think we should visit a certain bedroom," he said as he tugged. She stumbled up behind him, her coordination all shot to hell.

"The guest bedroom?" she asked and he realized that she was at least with it enough to make jokes.

"If you'd like," he teased. "I was thinking a bigger bed might be nice, though. A king, perhaps?"

"Ohhhh…for a king-sized guy?" she asked, laughing.

"You could say that." He'd let her judge size when they'd disrobed. Arizona was a long time ago, and she was a virgin at the time. She didn't have much experience to judge by last time.

They got to her bedroom door, and despite his teasing tone, Dawson realized that he really did feel special to be there. Last time she'd allowed him to get this far, he'd taken advantage of her on top of a pool table, he'd laughed at her gift to him, and then he'd walked away.

This time, he was going to make love to her. He was going to make her scream in delight.

He was going to make her *his*.

He'd stopped in the doorway and Chloe began to walk around him to get into the bedroom but he blocked her with his body. "Let me," he said, and scooped her up into his arms. She threw her arms around his neck and squealed in surprise.

"You should warn a girl before you do something like that," she said, laughing with delight. Her laughter belied her stern words, and he grinned down at her, feeling like he'd won some great prize. And he had. For Chloe to allow him back into her life was truly a wonderful prize.

He carried her, bouncing her up into the air a few times as he walked, listening to her squeal, pressing her body closer to his, and then once he got her to the bed, he dropped her. Bouncing across the bed, she howled, "Whaddya do that for?"

"'Cause all the *best* parts of you bounce when I do," he growled and, shucking his clothes as quickly as his fumbling fingers would allow him, he crawled across the bed towards her. She licked her lips in anticipation, looking him up and down as he moved towards her.

"Oh my," she sighed happily.

Which was pretty much all he had to say on the topic, too.

He clasped one foot and then the other in his hands, gently pulling her ballet slippers off her feet. Sensing his more serious, more sensual mood, her eyes darkened and then she leaned back against the pillows with a happy sigh.

Rather than moving up her legs, as he was sure she was expecting, he instead pulled her right foot up to his mouth and sucked on her big toe, laving the pad of it with his tongue.

"Whaaaaaaaa—" She gave a hoarse shout, and then the most *amazing* moans spilled out of her. Eyes closed, her back was arching and she began moaning, "Yes, please, yes, I didn't, ohh- hhhhh…" He moved down the most adorable row of toes he'd ever laid eyes on, and then across the arch of her foot. "Whaaaaaaaa—" she let out, the look of pure sexual gratification on her face as she did. God, she was sexy.

He didn't let up. He was going to make up for his earlier churlish behavior, even if it had taken him nine years to do it. Better late than never, right? He picked up her left foot and began nibbling on her perfect toes. Her back was arching and she was moaning and shaking and he hadn't even gotten to her calves yet.

Oh, it was going to be a good night tonight.

There was a certain looseness to her body and actions that he knew was a direct result of getting her drunk, which meant, his plan was working exactly as intended. He wanted her to stop thinking, to stop worrying, to just *be*. If he needed a little help in making that happen, well, he'd use that crutch.

This time.

"You know what I've always loved about your body?" he murmured as he began kissing his way up her calves. She thrashed on the bed and, well, it *looked* like she could be shaking her head, so he took that as her answer. "Your legs." He nibbled in circles around her kneecaps, one and then the other, and her moans hit a fevered pitch. Dawson stopped for just a moment to thank God Tommy wasn't home tonight. He was going to have to remember that Chloe was a moaner in bed.

A trait he would *happily* get used to.

He continued his move up her thighs, smooth and strong from years of waitressing, dancing, and cow milking. *What a combo...*

"They're so damn sexy. You should wear short skirts more often. Or short shorts." He reached the juncture of her thighs and began focusing his warm breath on her soft curls, slick with moisture. "You used to wear short shorts back at your dad's ranch. Oh, the daydreams I had about your legs," picked up one leg and draped it over his shoulder, "wrapping themselves," picked up the other leg and draped it over his other shoulder, "around my head and neck as I licked," he pursed his lips and sent a stream of cold air over her and she shivered, groaning as she did, "and sucked my way into an orgasm for you."

"Please, please, I...please..." she groaned, her eyes screwed tight, her head flipping on the pillow, her body shaking. "*Please.*"

He leaned down and *finally* pressed his lips against her, her sweet taste and moisture exploding across his tongue and he began his very best effort to make her forget her middle name. Or first name. Or any name at all, except for his. He liked the sound of his name on her lips.

"Ahhhhhrrrrrrgggghhhhhhh!" she half yelled, half moaned, as she arched her back, her body rigid, her legs shaking, and he tried to move with her, keeping his tongue moving over her, and she was shaking, shaking, shaking, until finally, her body collapsed into a boneless heap on the bed.

He grinned triumphantly. He was off to a

good start in terms of redeeming himself, if he did say so himself.

He moved over her, kissing his way up her delectable hip bones, her adorable innie belly button, her gorgeous breasts with a mole on the right one, reminding himself to go back and explore that more later, and finally, he was up to her mouth and was kissing her, and she was moaning again. He settled himself between her thighs, about to move inside, when he remembered.

Dammit, he *almost* got her pregnant again. Wouldn't that just be ironic. He rolled off her and went in search of his wallet, his hands shaking with need.

"Wha…" she asked drowsily, opening her eyes and trying to focus on him.

"I just need to keep Tommy 2 from arriving nine months from now," he said, chuckling as he rolled the rubber into place. Finally suited up, he moved between her thighs and this time, he was able to come home.

All of the traveling he'd done over the past nine years, and all of the places he'd gone, no

OVERDUE FOR LOVE | 165

one had felt as amazing as Chloe did. She was his north star. Sinking into her, he began thrusting, her warmth surrounding him, and he was so damn afraid he was going to make a fool out of himself by only lasting moments but she felt so damn good and it was almost impossible to hold himself back and then she was raising her hips, meeting every thrust with equal passion, equal vigor, and he was slamming in, his vision whiting out and he was coming, pumping, his back rigid as he spilled himself into her, unable to speak or think but only be.

It was endless and yet only moments, and then he was collapsing onto her with a happy sigh, nuzzling her neck, smiling against it.

He was finally home, and he was *never* going to leave again.

CHAPTER 15

CHLOE

CHLOE PULLED UP TO ADAM'S FARMHOUSE, unable to wipe the happy grin off her face. She felt…amazing. On top of the world. Better than ever.

She felt…whole.

She knocked on the front door out of politeness but then let herself in with a, "Hello!" This being Adam's mother's house, it had that certain grandma feel to it – lace and watercolors and porcelain cats abounding. Her house "fit" Adam much better, but Chloe sent up a silent thanks to the heavens that Adam was taking care of his mother and needed someone to stay in his house. She didn't know how she would've survived if she'd had to pay full rent on top of everything else.

"Mom!" Tommy cried, rounding the corner. He launched himself at her and she scooped him up into her arms, nuzzling his hair as she did so. Since he'd gotten older, he didn't let her hug him as much, but apparently, staying the night with Adam knocked down his "I'm a big boy" philosophy just a smidge.

"Hey, Chloe," Adam said, coming in from the kitchen. She heard his mom warble, "Hi, Chloe!" and she shouted back, "Hi, Ruby!"

Adam searched her face and then…his face dropped and she could tell something was wrong. "Adam?" she asked hesitantly. "What's wrong?"

He forced a smile onto his face that was so patently fake, it was pretty much the smile version of turf grass. "Oh nothing!" he said with a chuckle that sounded like it got stuck in his throat. Tommy, who'd wiggled his way out of Chloe's arms, began tugging on her.

"Mom, let's go!" he said excitedly. He was

obviously over his stomach bug, that was for damn sure.

"Well, thanks again for watching Tommy last night," Chloe said to Adam, feeling weirdly formal with her best friend. He was just acting so…stiff.

"Anytime," Adam said, and he *almost* sounded like he meant that statement. He turned to Tommy and his whole face brightened, his golden brown eyes lighting up from within like she was used to seeing. It was…disconcerting. "And I want *you* to come over soon and ride horses with me. Ladybug really needs to spend more time with you if I'm going to train her for use in the therapy camp. A lot of those kids have never been around horses, not like you. She needs to spend time around a kid with horse smarts."

"Oh yes!" Tommy crowed excitedly. Adam might as well have handed Tommy a giant three-layer cake and told him to eat the whole thing by himself. She was impressed by Adam's deft ability at making Tommy feel special and needed. It was a talent, truly.

"Anything further on that front?" Chloe asked, ignoring Tommy's tugs on her arm.

"Just trying to find a bank to help with the backing of it so I can expand it. Right now, it's in the beta phase," Adam said, his face stiff again, his turf-grass smile firmly plastered back into place.

"Well, tell me what I can do to help to really get it off the ground. I'd love to help however I can."

"Thanks," he said, nodding his head.

As they headed out the front door and into the bright morning sunshine, Tommy went on about everything they'd done together, which included eating dinner, brushing the horses, and playing a card game Adam taught Tommy. Apparently, Tommy was a whiz at the game and won every single round they played. Chloe hid her grin. That was Adam, all right – a good guy to the very last drop.

So why was he so weird this morning?

When they got back home, Tommy bounded out of the car in search of Dawson, and found him in the chicken coop, fixing that old hinge that'd been broken for the last three months. She'd kept meaning to say something to Adam but it wasn't a huge deal and Adam had a lot on his plate. She really should've just tackled the job herself but…well, she also had a lot on her plate.

As she watched him work the screwdriver, listening to Tommy tell him all about his night with Adam, she couldn't help smiling. It was… nice. It was like they were a real family. As if Dawson could hear her thoughts, he looked up at her and winked, "ummming" and "ohh-hing" to Tommy all the while.

"Can I put the next screw in?" Tommy asked excitedly.

"Let me get it started for you," Dawson said, pushing the tip of the screw into the wood and then rotating the screwdriver a few times to push it into place.

Stepping away, Chloe headed to the house. Someone had to make breakfast 'round here, and Dawson had already taken his turn. She needed some way to thank him for all of his hard work and patience and…lovemaking.

Her smile to herself grew wider. She'd have to cook a *lot* of breakfasts to thank him for that.

Their Saturday passed in a sweet blur. Tommy reported his screwdriver feats as they ate breakfast together, and then Dawson left with Tommy for the rodeo, simply giving Chloe a wink as they left. She appreciated his understanding in not kissing her in front of Tommy. She wanted this with him, but...she wasn't ready to jump in with both feet. Not yet. It had only been a few days and...

Well, she just wasn't ready, that was all. Thank God Dawson seemed to understand this without her having to spell it out in giant red letters.

Having the house to herself was weirdly thrilling and lonely. She was used to spending Saturdays with Tommy, trying to convince him that making his bed was not akin to child slavery, while she cleaned and prepped for the week. Then they'd spend their afternoons down at the creek, catching bullfrogs or going for walks in the woods or even driving over to Sawyer Lake to splash in the water.

She found that today, she was so much more efficient without an eight year old underfoot – strange how that works – but a part of her was also…sad.

She shook her head and went back to work, scrubbing the shelves in the fridge that she'd been neglecting for a long time. She wasn't about to moon over having the day to herself, not after wishing for exactly this for years. She loved Tommy, but even moms needed breaks every once in a while.

CHAPTER 16

CHLOE

RIGHT AND *WAY* TOO EARLY on Sunday morning, Dawson snuck out of bed and down the hallway to the guest bedroom. After Tommy had gone to bed last night, he'd come in and they'd made love for what seemed like hours. This was a habit she could easily fall into. Her body, starved of love and affection for years, soaked up his attention like a desert flower in a spring rainstorm. Considerate enough to leave her before Tommy awoke, Chloe had to be content with simply snuggling his pillow close to her and breathing in his scent. He smelled so damn good – almost as good as he kissed.

She rolled over with a groan. She was turning into a horny teenager all over again. She hadn't truly known what being with Dawson would be like when she'd chased him for two years. She'd only known that she wanted him with every fiber of her being. If she'd known what sleeping with him would actually feel like, she would've wanted him with every fiber *and* breath in her body.

With a contented smile, she drifted off to sleep.

"Mom, wake up," Tommy said, shaking her shoulder.

"Wha…?" she asked, slowly opening up her eyes and trying to focus on her son's face. "What's wrong?" she slurred.

"Dawson said to wake you up – that it was time for breakfast!" His job done, he clattered out of the room and down the stairs.

Breakfast? He made us breakfast again? God, please don't ever let him leave. Ever.

After an amazing breakfast of fluffy scrambled eggs and links of sausage, Chloe took Tommy to day camp and then headed to work. Her one day off a week – Saturday – was over. It was back to work for her. Dawson stayed at the farm, saying he had some projects he could work on. She'd never met anyone with such get-up-and-go before. It was…

Blissful.

Which was exactly how the next few days felt to her. Blissful. She could live in this fantasy world of Dawson playing the part of her husband for as long as the world would let her. She hadn't been this content in…well, ever, actually. This was a world she'd wanted to live in ever since she'd met Mr. Dawson Blackhorse, and after years of difficulties, she was finally seeing that dream come true.

And then, Friday night, she came home, Tommy in tow, not finding Dawson out in the barn, fixing the roof or cleaning out the stalls, not in the kitchen with a towel slung over his shoulder, but instead in the guest bedroom, slinging his clothes into his duffel bag.

"What are…" Chloe ground to a halt.

Whatever was going on, Tommy shouldn't be there for it. "Hey, why don't you go check on Bolt?" she told Tommy in her I'm-not-asking-I'm-telling-you voice. With a glance of confusion between his parents, Tommy wheeled around and clattered down the stairs and out the back door, the screen door slamming against the frame as he went. Chloe grimaced, making a mental note to talk to her son *again* about how to exit a house, and then turned back to Dawson, who was still angrily stuffing things into his bag.

"Wanna tell me what this is all about?" she asked, arms crossed as she stared at him. She leaned against the four-poster bed, a gorgeous, antique relic left behind by Adam, and waited for Dawson to speak.

Silence. Dawson stopped shoving things into the duffel bag but he just stared down at it, not speaking, not moving, and certainly, not looking her in the eye.

She could outlast him though. She was as stubborn as Ivy.

"You two don't need me," he finally said into the silence.

"Don't…what are you talking about?"

"You don't need me. I'm only useful when it comes to sneaking into your room at night, and fixing things around the farm. You're treating me like your dad did – a farm hand, but you're kind enough to dole a little somethin' out on the side."

"Are you being serious right now?" she asked, trying to keep her voice level. Calm.

Even though she really wanted to take his lasso and whack him upside the head a few dozen times.

When he didn't answer, when he just continued staring down at his duffel bag, she asked him, "What is this really about? What's going on?"

"Every day this week, you took Tommy to day camp. Every day after day camp ended, Adam picked him up and had him hang out with him on vet trips. Every afternoon, you met up with Adam and got Tommy from him to bring home to me. Here. *Not* to me – I'm an after-thought." His voice broke and so he stopped talking for a moment, just breathing deeply, and then he continued, his voice a little softer. "Has it ever occurred to *anyone* that I might want to spend my day with Tommy?"

Finally, oh God *finally*, he turned and looked at her, pleading. "He's my son and yet, in so many ways, he's a stranger to me. I don't even know what his favorite color is!"

"Green," she supplied without thinking. When he just stared at her, she shrugged. "Like grass in the springtime. He loves it."

"I didn't know that," he whispered, staring at her, his eyes haunted. "I've spent this whole week, waiting for someone to notice that I can be a father, too. That maybe *I* can pick up Tommy from day camp. That maybe, he doesn't have to go at all. I could be teaching him so many things – how to exercise a horse. How to swing a hammer. How to milk an ornery old goat. Instead, I'm left here. By my-self. Just to think and fix Adam's shit for him."

"Adam's…did something happen between you two?" When Dawson's eyes shifted and he stared over her shoulder at the far wall, she knew she'd hit on something. Something painful. Something he definitely did not want to talk about.

Which just made her more determined to cover every square inch of it.

"What's going on between you and Adam?" she asked. "Have you guys talked when I wasn't around?"

Dawson massaged his right earlobe, a sure sign of stress and then shrugged. "He came over yesterday to fix the hinge on the chicken coop. I guess he'd seen it and had been meaning to come over and do it for a while but just hadn't gotten around to it. He was surprised and…not real happy that I'd already fixed it.

"Chloe, he's in love with you." His voice broke and his eyes met hers as his fingers rubbed his lobe harder. "I can see it in his eyes, in his gestures…no man under the age of a hundred could resist you, and I promise you, Adam is much younger than one hundred."

She couldn't help breaking out into laughter. "Adam, in love with me?" she said between gasps. "Oh, Dawson…" She wiped at her eyes and then straightened. She had to look him straight in the eye when she said this so he could see how serious she was.

"Adam is my friend, nothing more. We have always been friends. You can't deliver a baby in a snowstorm in the back seat of a pickup truck without becoming friends for life. He saved my life that night – the life of Tommy and me. And he's saved it many times over since then, by letting me rent this house for free, by helping me take care of Tommy. I will *always* be in his debt.

"But I am not in love with him. And I don't think he's in love with me. And—" she held up a hand to forestall the argument about to spill out of Dawson, "—even if he is, love is a two-way street. He and I will never be more than best friends. Period. Whatever he wants beyond that, is on him. I cannot help him out with it.

"Not when I'm in love with you."

The ticking of the clock was the only sound as she held her breath, eyes searching his. What would he say? What if she'd made a fool out of herself?

He smiled then, a painful, happy, joyous, tortured smile. "Really?" he breathed. "But Chloe, I screwed up all that time ago. I really made a mess of it. I don't expect you to forgive me for years for that mistake, and if you need all of that time to find it in your heart to forgive me, I'll take it as penance. I just want to be in your life in the meanwhile. I want to be a father to Tommy, I want to be your one and only. I want you to think of me when it's time to make plans for the day. I want you to include me in your life. In Tommy's life. And someday, I want you to forgive me for being a jackass."

She pulled away from the bedpost and moved to his side, running her fingers through his long, silky hair. "And I want *you* to talk to me. In Arizona, nine years ago, you thought I'd done this horrible crime, and you didn't stop. You didn't ask. You just assumed. And today, you were doing the same thing. You thought that you *knew* how I felt about Adam. You have to talk to me, Dawson Blackhorse."

"But I did ask you," he said, defending himself even as he pulled her close against him. She listened to his heartbeat through his button-up shirt, snuggling close, even as they continued to argue. *I think we should fight all arguments just like this.* It seemed like a damn good idea.

"When did you ask me?" She could not remember him bringing that topic up. She would've told him.

"The night after I ran into you at the diner. In the kitchen, remember? You wouldn't tell me anything except that you guys have a cozy relationship."

Okay, maybe snuggling him while fighting wouldn't work after all. She had to look him in the eye to see if he was being serious.

Shit. He was.

"Dawson," she said, her voice as serious as could be, "you asked me when I was still bloody pissed at you. Of *course* I wasn't going to tell you anything. You were jealous of Adam with *no* right to be. I hadn't seen you in years and you had no right to ask me what I'd been doing or who I'd been sleeping with. I'm not entirely sure I would've told you my favorite color that night if you'd asked me. I—"

"What is it?" he interrupted, pulling her back against his chest and stroking her hair.

"Purple. Deep, royal purple. Like the edges of a sunset."

"Thank you."

"You're welcome. And," she added, her head snuggled against his chest, "aren't you going to miss the rodeo world? Rex is going on to Montana, so it isn't like the Stampede is the last event of the season. It's only August! Even I know that rodeos last into September, at least."

He ran his fingers through her hair again and again, and she knew it was a mindless gesture while he thought through his answer.

"That afternoon at the diner – I was already thinking about how this was going to be it for me, at least for a while. Being on the road is hard on a person. I didn't know where I was going after this, and had thought I'd spend some time while here, considering my options. I have to admit, in all the options I ran through in my head, spending time with you and a long-lost son was not on my list." His chuckle reverberated through her head and she smiled contentedly, refusing to move away from his warm embrace.

"I've been saving up money for a long time. With the seed money from...Arizona, I was able to parlay into cash prizes at rodeos. I have a knack for calf roping. I have a knack for goat milking." She laughed at that.

"But my dream is horse breeding. That's why I wanted the Bartell Ranch so badly, I was willing to buy it from a bigoted asshole."

"Hey, don't say things like that! You're insulting the bigoted assholes of the world!"

He burst out laughing and she pulled back in his arms to saucily grin up at him.

"The truth is, the rodeo world was just a way for me to make money – something I knew I could do without having to put on a coat and tie every day. But it isn't my passion. It never has been."

It was quiet for a moment, and then Dawson dropped a kiss on the crown of her head. He pulled away and dropped to one knee in front of her.

Oh no, please don't do that – I'm not read—

"Chloe Joy Bartell, will you date me?" he asked, pulling her hands to his chest. "We've done everything backwards so far – first we made a child together, then I made you raise that child alone, then we lived and slept together. We need to go back to the beginning. I'm going to get a place in town, I'm going to move in there, and I'm going to date you like a real man should've from the beginning. I'm *not* going to sneak into your room at night like an unwanted thief. We're going to date and fall in love.

"Will you go steady with me?" His dark brown eyes stared up at her and she felt her own filling with tears.

"Yes, Dawson Blackhorse, I will go steady with you," she whispered, joy filling her soul.

He stood and wrapped his arms around

her, pulling her tight against him, and began kissing her, kissing her tears away.

"Oh, and Dawson?"

"Yes?" he asked, nuzzling her neck.

"Thanks for asking this time."

He pulled back and smiled down at her.

"Always."

CHAPTER 17

CHLOE

THEY STARTED THE ADVENTURE on a beautiful autumn Friday afternoon. The sun shone brightly overhead, lighting up the brilliant blue sky, but thankfully, the heat of summer had finally passed. The orange and brown leaves swirled down from the quaking aspen trees as they followed the curves of the mountain road.

Tommy was practically vibrating with excitement in the backseat of Dawson's Ford. Chloe could totally relate, unable to sit still herself. Her excitement had little to do with a day of hiking, fishing, or any other camping-related activities, though. It was just so damn nice to spend the weekend together as a family. She'd even asked Betty for Sunday off, so they could spend two nights out in the wilderness together.

It didn't take long to reach Eagle Rock State Park. She was glad to have Dawson there to help put up the tents. She was capable of putting up tents herself, of course, but it had always taken a long time, which made Tommy antsy while frustrating her. It was great to see someone else deal with an antsy eight year old instead of her.

With a grin, she watched as Dawson showed their son how to put up the tents, patiently walking him through each step. It was hard for Tommy to concentrate, considering the fact that Dawson had promised him a fishing trip that day, but finally, Dawson told Tommy quietly that either he helped with setting up the tents and truly concentrated on the task at hand, or they wouldn't go fishing after all.

Oh, what a difference from the Dawson just two months earlier, who hadn't been able to tell

Tommy no at the rodeo. Tommy immediately put his mind to the task and they finally got the tents erected.

After they finished setting up camp, everyone grabbed their fishing poles and headed down to the lake to fish. An osprey swooped and dove overhead as they cast from the bank, and they watched in awe with only a little bit of grumbling at how many fish the bird was catching, compared to their pathetic haul. Tommy and Chloe ended up netting one fish each, but none for Dawson.

"You get to clean them," she said with a grin, passing the bucket to him. With some good-natured grumbling, he took the fish to the cleaning station and proved he was adept at that task, too.

They headed back to camp where she set about preparing dinner. The backup cooler of food, filled with red potatoes, veggies, and condiments, helped round out their meal. Afterward, they sat around the small fire in the fire pit and roasted marshmallows. This time, she watched Dawson keep an eye on Tommy's intake of sweets, and was happy to see that Tommy was listening to Dawson just like he did to Chloe.

She kept waiting for him to start trying to play Dawson and her off each other, but so far, he hadn't. She loved seeing Tommy snuggle up to his father, arms around each other as they competed on who could roast their marshmallows to a golden brown *without* setting them on fire.

Yup, he truly was a "mini me" to his dad.

"Next time, we'll have to bring some ATVs and hit the trails," said Dawson to Tommy, ruffling his hair. Tears pricked her eyes when she imagined how different their life could've been if she'd been able to find him before their son was born.

With a sigh, she pushed away the melancholy thought, knowing there was no use dwelling on what might have been. It was time to concentrate on the future, and more specifically, their sleeping arrangements that night. Tommy hadn't batted an eyelash when Dawson had told him that he was going to sleep with his mom that night. It was the first time they were going to openly sleep together around Tommy, but he'd taken it like a pro. Tommy'd fallen in love with Dawson almost as much as she had, listening to everything he had to say, following him everywhere he went.

It tugged at her heart strings to think about it.

Tommy started yawning and was coaxed into going to bed with the promise of a sunrise walk with Dawson.

"*I'll* be sleeping in," she said, grinning. Tommy didn't grumble but instead, kissed her on the cheek and headed to the tent with a mumbled "Goodnight," as he went.

His soft snores emerged from the tent soon after, leaving them virtually alone. She scooted her chair closer to Dawson's and put her hand on his thigh. "I'm so glad we're doing this."

"Me too." He shook his head. "He's amazing, isn't he?"

"I've always thought so." She winked at him. "He's a lot like his father."

He didn't pick up on her lighthearted mood. "That must've been tough to handle."

Her brows furrowed when she frowned. "What?"

"Having him look like me when you hated me so much."

Chloe sighed. "I don't think I ever hated you, Dawson, although the sentence 'A virgin who has no idea how to please a man' was one that I had to go to therapy to get over." He began to apologize again, but she waved it away. "Yeah, I was hurt, and my confidence took a beating, but I couldn't hate you. I definitely couldn't regret that Tommy looked and acted so much like you. He's a terrific little boy, with a pretty terrific dad."

Dawson slipped his arm around her shoulders, pulling her as close as the camping chairs would allow. "His mom is damned special, too."

Slowly, she trailed her hand higher up his thigh, pausing near the juncture. The material of his jeans strained under her hand as he hardened.

With a groan, he put his hand over hers, arresting her ascent. "You should stop now, Chloe."

"Or what?" she asked in a husky drawl.

Their gazes locked, silently speaking of mutual hunger. "If you don't stop, I won't be able to, and that will blow the hell out of my plan to just sit around the fire and talk to you as the wood burns down."

"I'm tired of talking." She pushed her hand higher, easily circumventing his halfhearted attempt to stop her. "We can watch the fire burn tomorrow night, promise." Another groan signaled his surrender as she reached her destination, cupping the length of him and stroking through the well-worn denim.

He jerked away from her hand and stood. She didn't protest when he pulled her from her chair. Chloe twined her fingers through his and led him to their tent. As soon as they were inside, and he'd zipped up the mosquito flap, he took her in his arms. She lifted her head, straining to touch his lips to hers.

He lowered his mouth to meet hers while

gathering her even closer. The kiss started out slow and gentle, but she shifted restlessly, pushing her tongue inside to taste him. Their tongues caressed each other. She stroked his, swirling around his mouth and eliciting another groan. His thick hair was silky between her fingers when she plunged a hand into the depths to drag him closer. Right then, she wanted to be part of him.

They shared a hungry kiss, each eager to merge with the other. She strained against him, bringing her hands to the hem of his t-shirt to push it up. His skin beckoned before she'd accomplished the task of removing the shirt, so she left the fabric bunched under his arms as she stroked his taut stomach. The dusting of hair tickled her fingers, and she scratched him lightly. Dawson hissed, his breath a harsh exhalation against her lips.

She didn't resist when he grasped her hand to pull it away from his stomach. He held it in his, trapped between their bodies. Undeterred, she brought her free hand to the waistband of his jeans, tugging at the snap and starting on the zipper before he intercepted that hand. She looked at him through the veil of her lashes as he held her hands captive in his. "You're not making this easy."

A throaty chuckle vibrated in his chest. "You're making it too easy, babe. If you don't slow down, it won't be any fun for you."

"I disagree." She tugged lightly, and he released her hands. With a shrug of surrender, Dawson stripped off his shirt. As he lowered his hands to take off his jeans, she took advantage of the moment to remove her tank top and khaki shorts. By the time she started to undo her bra, he was naked. Chloe stopped when he put up a hand, dropping hers to her side.

Dawson undid the front clasp of her bra with a steady hand, but the ragged sigh he released at the sight of her breasts spilling free betrayed he wasn't as unruffled as he pretended to be. Chloe lost her own battle to maintain a cool façade when he cupped her breasts, his thumbs teasing her already tight nipples into rigid peaks. She arched her back and tossed her head when he lowered his mouth to taste one.

She grasped his hair, pulling him closer as he sucked one nipple before turning his head to pay equal attention to the other. As one, they dropped to the sleeping bag, with Dawson on top of her. His mouth never left her breast as they settled into place. Grasping his shoulders, she held on to her tenuous control, remembering the necessity to be quiet as he lowered his head, licking a trail down her belly.

It took every ounce of control not to cry out when he nestled his face against the crotch of her silken panties, inhaling her scent. She squirmed, eager to open up to him, as Dawson darted out his tongue to taste her through the fabric. "Please," she rasped. Could she die from sensual torment? If he didn't give her more soon, she was about to find out.

With a low chuckle, Dawson grasped the elastic of her panties between his teeth and pulled them down to her thighs. She was trapped, unable to open her legs more than a couple of inches, but that was enough. His warm tongue slipped inside her, making her bite hard on her lip to stifle the shout that wanted to escape when his tongue touched her slippery nub.

He spent several minutes exploring her contours, finding each of the delicious places that made her writhe and want to scream with pleasure. Chloe stuffed her hand into her mouth to hold in her cries when he sucked her into his mouth while simultaneously thrusting two fingers into her slick folds. Her body yielded to his masterful touch, and she arched against him, tossing her head to keep quiet.

The orgasm broke over her before she realized it was happening, her arms flinging wide, back arching, and she would've screamed if Dawson hadn't clamped a hand over her mouth to muffle the sound. She twisted and shuddered under the force of release, all the while knowing it was a pale imitation of how she would feel when their bodies fused together and she once again trembled on the brink of climax.

As if he'd read her mind, Dawson moved his hand to strip away her panties. He nestled between her thighs and she was thankful once again that she'd gone on birth control and they no longer had to have a barrier between them.

As he sank inside her slick heat, she welcomed every inch of him. He moved gently within her, easing in his full length before withdrawing to repeat the process, and it was as if the past nine years had truly melted away, once and for all – disappearing into the cleansing mountain air. They were once again on the pool table, making love for the first time, but this time, without the anger between them.

Dawson stroked her nub as he quickened his pace. Chloe met each thrust with equal vigor, longing to reach fulfillment with him at the same time. Her orgasm hovered on the edge of her consciousness, and she deliberately staved it off until he stiffened, his arms trembling as he held himself above her. Feeling him spasm within her, she gave up her own weak control and surrendered to her release, letting go and falling into the abyss with him.

Afterward, they lay curled together in the darkness, Dawson kissing her forehead and cheek. "I love you, Chloe. I have for a long time, but I cocked it up and forced myself to pretend like you'd never meant anything to me." He shifted enough so their gazes locked in the dim light. "You probably won't believe it, but I thought about coming back to the ranch more than once in the weeks after I left. I thought you'd betrayed me, but I still wanted you."

She sighed. "I wish you had. Maybe you could've found me before Tommy was born, and we wouldn't have lost all these years." Chloe pushed a stray strand of hair out of his eyes. "And...I love you, too." She breathed the words into the quiet night air, her heart thrilling that she could finally speak them out loud.

They hadn't said those words to each other since that night in August, when he'd thought he had to leave her behind, that he wasn't a wanted part of their lives.

To finally say those words to each other on a night like tonight – gorgeous and fulfilling and touching...it meant the world to Chloe. *Dawson* meant the world to Chloe.

Snuggled up against his side, his arm wrapped around her shoulder, she drifted off into a contented sleep, listening to the crickets chirp and the owls hoot their way through the darkness.

EPILOGUE

DAWSON

Seven Months Later
May, 2018

*D*AWSON MADE THE LAST TURN of their journey, knowing that they were almost there, and that neither Chloe nor Tommy knew where they were going. He was part nervous, part excited, part ready to throw up.

God, please…

He left the prayer unfinished as the farmhouse came into view. He looked over at Chloe, grinning. "We're almost there," he told her.

"Oh, good!" she said, starting to take off the blindfold.

"No, no, no!" he said, slapping her hands away from the fabric. "No cheating!"

Tommy was bouncing ecstatically in the back seat. "C'mon, Dad," he said cajolingly, "can't we just peek?"

Even as Dawson's heart contracted with love over the word "Dad" – he would *never* tire of hearing his son call him that – he held firm. "Nope, no peeking for you!" Tommy groaned in pain, but Dawson ignored it.

He wasn't going to screw this up. After all this time, he was going to get it right.

He stopped in front of the house and cut the engine. "Ladies and gentlemen," he said dramatically, "I give you...the Blackhorse Ranch!"

They tore their blindfolds off and squealed in perfect unison. If he hadn't known any better, he would've thought they had practiced that.

"Oh, Dad!" Tommy said, throwing the back

door open and scrambling out of the truck. "It's awesome!" Chloe and Dawson climbed out after him and watched as he tore down to the creek that ran through the backyard.

"This is so cool!" he hollered back as he knelt down in the mud on the creek bank.

"I think you're going to have laundry to do tonight," Dawson said dryly, watching the giant brown blotches on his son's clothing grow in size as he lay on his stomach and tried to catch fish as they swam by.

Chloe just laughed. "I am the mother of a 9-year-old boy. I think I have laundry to do *every* night."

He slipped his arm around her waist.

"So come check out the house," he said eagerly. "It has four bedrooms and two bathrooms! One bathroom has been remodeled, and one…most definitely has not." He slipped a key into the lock and pushed the front door open, leading into a beautiful living room with original hardwood floors and leaded glass windows. "It was built in 1882," he said proudly.

"The Miller family built it, so it's one of the first in the area."

She gasped with delight as she fingered one of the massive wooden columns that connected to a bookcase, splitting the living room in half. "Oh Dawson, it's gorgeous. You know how much I love original woodwork like this. And you bought it?!" She turned to him in surprise. "When? How did I not know this?!"

"Because I wanted to surprise you. For once, I wanted to not talk to you about something that I was doing that was wonderful, instead of only clamming up when it came to the shitty stuff."

She laughed, the happy sound spilling out of her as she admired the fireplace mantel.

"I do have to say, I much prefer positive surprises that you've kept to yourself, as opposed to the other times, when you just assumed you knew what I was thinking or feeling, and didn't bother asking to make sure."

"Somehow, I thought so. Just a wild guess…" he said with a grin, grabbing her hand and pulling her into the remodeled kitchen so she could ooh and aahh over that, too. "The house has four bedrooms and two bathrooms," he said, a little too casually, as she pulled the oven door open to inspect it and turned the water tap on and off in the kitchen sink.

"Yeah," she said distractedly, looking at the inside of the fridge. "I think you should look at having the seal around the edge of the door re-placed though. This isn't a real tight fit and you'll lose cold air out of it."

He tried to swallow his laughter and his nerves. "I'll definitely get right on that," he promised, while she headed down the hallway to the remodeled bathroom. Done up in blues and creams, with a chair rail and beadboard around the bottom 2/3s of the walls, it was peaceful and beautiful and exactly what he wanted in a house.

In a *home*.

He tried again.

"So, did I mention that there are four bed-rooms and two bathrooms?" he asked, a little desperate this time. She stopped inspecting the toilet seal on her hands and knees and instead stood to stare at him.

"Dawson Blackhorse, either you think I've gone deaf or senile or both. You've told me that there are four bedrooms and two bathrooms in this house three times now. Are you really excited about having an office or something?"

Finally, the moment had come and yeah, maybe he hadn't expected to do it in the bathroom but hell, they never had done anything normal. Why start now?

He dropped to one knee, fumbling with the ring box but finally getting it pointed the right way, *and* open. A miracle, considering how much his hands were shaking.

"Chloe Joy Bartell," he said, his heart in his throat, "I want to marry you and give you a hundred more sons and daughters and start a horse breeding ranch and make you mine. Will you be mine?"

She gasped and covered her mouth with her hands, staring at him for a moment and he couldn't breathe and then she laughed, tears streaming down her face as she did so. "I was always yours," she breathed happily, throwing herself at him and knocking him backwards onto the cold tile floor, "but we may need to have a discussion about a hundred children. I really don't think four bedrooms will house that many kids, for starters, and—"

He kissed her then, knowing that he could listen to her practicalities later. For now, he had a wife-to-be to kiss, and the way he figured it, he was way overdue for a little love in his life.

"Ewwwww…" Tommy said from the doorway of the bathroom. "On the bathroom floor? Seriously."

Scrambling off Dawson, Chloe only grinned at their son, no embarrassment in her eyes. "Someday, you'll understand," she promised him.

Someday, he would.

ALSO BY ERIN WRIGHT

~ LONG VALLEY ~

~ FIREFIGHTERS OF LONG VALLEY ~

Flames of Love

Inferno of Love

Fire and Love

Burned by Love

~ MUSICIANS OF LONG VALLEY ~

Strummin' Up Love

Melody of Love (TBA)

Rock 'N Love (TBA)

Rhapsody of Love (TBA)

~ SERVICEMEN OF LONG VALLEY ~

Thankful for Love (2021)

Commanded to Love (TBA)

Salute to Love (TBA)

Harbored by Love (TBA)

ABOUT ERIN WRIGHT

USA TODAY BESTSELLING AUTHOR ERIN WRIGHT has worked every job under the sun, including library director, barista, teacher, website designer, and ranch hand helping brand cattle, before settling into the career she's always dreamed about: Author.

She still loves coffee, doesn't love the smell of cow flesh burning, and has embarked on the adventure of a lifetime, traveling the country full-time in an RV. (No one has died yet in the confined 250-square-foot space – which she considers a real win – but let's be real, next week isn't looking so good...)

Find her updates on ErinWright.net, where you can sign up for her newsletter along with the requisite pictures of Jasmine the Writing

Cat, her kitty cat muse and snuggle buddy extraordinaire.

Wanna get in touch?
www.erinwright.net
erin@erinwright.net

Or reach out to Erin on your favorite social media platform:

facebook.com/AuthorErinWright

twitter.com/erinwrightlv

pinterest.com/erinwrightbooks

goodreads.com/erinwright

bookbub.com/profile/erin-wright

instagram.com/authorerinwright

CPSIA information can be obtained
at www.ICGtesting.com
Printed in the USA
LVHW081806281122
734200LV00031B/1312